A virgin! He  believe it.

How could a girl loo... responding as she did to a man's touch, reach almost twenty-two without having intimately known a male body?

Presents™

Passion™

**Looking for sophisticated stories that sizzle?
Wanting a read that has a little extra spice?**

**Pick up a Presents Passion™—
where seduction is *guaranteed!***

**Look out for our next Passion title in July,
by favorite author
Emma Darcy
#2038, The Secret Mistress**

MIRANDA LEE

The Millionaire's Mistress

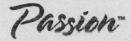

Passion™

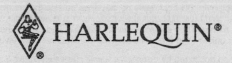

HARLEQUIN®

TORONTO • NEW YORK • LONDON
AMSTERDAM • PARIS • SYDNEY • HAMBURG
STOCKHOLM • ATHENS • TOKYO • MILAN • MADRID
PRAGUE • WARSAW • BUDAPEST • AUCKLAND

ISBN 0-373-12026-5

THE MILLIONAIRE'S MISTRESS

First North American Publication 1999.

CHAPTER ONE

HE WATCHED her from the safety of distance, annoyed with himself for watching her at all.

She was cavorting in the pool with a group of young bucks, revelling in their admiration, flirting outrageously with all of them.

He couldn't take his eyes off her any more than they could, his narrowed gaze captivated by that long tawny blonde hair, those flashing blue eyes and that lushly laughing mouth.

The laughter died on her lips when one of the young men playfully pulled her under the water. She came up spluttering, struggling to push the mass of thick wet hair out of her face. Whirling away from her admirers, she swam with petulant strokes over to the ladder, where she hauled herself upwards, her nose in the air, water cascading from her curves—her perfectly proportioned, glisteningly gorgeous curves.

Once out of the pool, she flipped her hair over and slowly wrung it out like a towel, bending forward as she did so, her breasts almost spilling out of her bikini top, which was slightly askew.

He cursed as he felt his flesh automatically respond. She was everything he desired—and despised. A high-spirited, high-class rich bitch, with beauty to burn, a body to die for, and a soul undoubtedly as spoilt and selfish as sin.

He didn't know her name. He didn't need to. It

would be something like Tiffany, or Felicity.
Maybe Jacqueline. Perhaps even another Stephany.

Her name didn't matter. *She* didn't matter. What
mattered was that he wasn't yet immune to her type.

God, would he never learn?

His sigh was weary. He should not have come.
This sort of empty partying was not for him. He'd
grown past it. He wanted more these days. And he
wouldn't find more here.

Putting his drink down on a nearby table, he
turned from the window and went in search of his
host.

'But the night's still young!' Felix exclaimed
when his esteemed guest said his goodbyes.

'Sorry,' he returned. 'It's been a long week.'

'You work too hard at that bank of yours.'

'Undoubtedly.'

'You should learn to relax more, Marcus,' came
the unwelcome advice. 'Why not stay a little while
longer? Have another drink and I'll introduce you
to the Montgomery girl.'

'The Montgomery girl?'

'Justine Montgomery. I saw you watching her a
moment ago. Not that I blame you. She's a peach.
Ripe and ready for the picking.'

Justine...

Yes, that suited. It had a snooty air to it, just like
its owner. As for her being ripe and ready for the
picking... Marcus only just managed to suppress a
cynical laugh. He had no illusions about the Justine
Montgomerys of this world. The odds were she'd
been picked from the tree many years before.
Picked and handled and devoured in every way possible.

He'd met plenty of Justines over the past ten years or so. He'd even married one.

A small shudder ran through him at the memory.

'I don't think so, Felix. Girls like Miss Montgomery are best admired from a distance.'

'Don't let your marriage to Stephany sour you. Not all women are as fickle or as faithless as her.'

'Thank God for that. Though I would hardly categorise Miss Montgomery as a woman. She doesn't look a day over twenty-one.'

'That's because she isn't. But so what if she's young? Stephany was only twenty-one when you married her, wasn't she?'

'Exactly,' came his dry reply.

'You don't have to marry the girl, you know.'

'Oh, yes, I know that. Only too well.'

'That's not what I meant. Don't judge the daughter by the father. Grayson Montgomery might be amoral, but Justine's a very sweet girl.'

Marcus' laughter was cold and hard. 'Too sweet for me, I think. I like my peaches a little less…er… ripe. Still, if I ever run into Miss Montgomery again, I'll remember your recommendation. Now, I really must go. I have a board meeting first thing tomorrow morning.'

Justine parked her silver Nissan 200SX Sports in the double garage, and zapped the roll-down door shut behind her. Her father's car space was empty and she frowned. Where on earth could he be at midnight on a Sunday night?

A Saturday night would have been different. He played poker with his racing buddies most Saturday nights, to all hours of the morning. It was not unknown for him to stay out all night, going straight to his Sunday golf game without returning home.

But Sunday evening he usually reserved for his wife. Still frowning, Justine scooped up her carryall from the passenger seat and ran up the back stairs to the first floor of the house—and the bedrooms. Seeing the light on under her mother's door, she stopped and knocked softly.

'Mum? Are you awake?'

'Yes, darling. Come on in.'

Adelaide Montgomery was perched up in bed against a mountain of pillows, a blockbuster novel in one hand and a half-eaten chocolate in the other. At fifty-seven, Justine's mother was still a very attractive lady, meticulous with her hair and face. But her once hourglass figure had succumbed to more than middle-age spread over the past few years or so. She was always bemoaning her increased weight, blaming it on everything from early menopause to hormone replacement therapy.

'Mum, you naughty lady,' Justine reproached when she saw the large box of chocolates beside the bed. 'You're supposed to be starting a diet this week.'

'And so I am, darling. Tomorrow.'

'Daddy not home yet?' Justine asked, levering herself up onto the end of her parents' huge fourposter bed.

'No, he's not. And I'm going to have a word with him when he does come too. When he rang to let me know he wouldn't be home for dinner, he could have indicated he might be this late. Just as well I'm not a worrier.'

Which she wasn't, Justine conceded. Her mother

never worried about anything because she never took responsibility for anything. Grayson Montgomery was the head of the Montgomery family in every way. He ran the household, hired and fired staff, made all the decisions and paid all the bills. Neither mother nor daughter knew much about his business dealings, other than the fact he ran a high-powered financial consultancy and worked very long hours.

A handsome and charismatic man, Grayson spoilt his wife and daughter shamelessly in material things, but, in truth, didn't spend much time with either of them. Never had.

Justine sometimes wondered what sort of relationship her older brother would have had with his father—had he lived. But Adelaide Montgomery's firstborn hadn't lived. Her beloved little Lorne had died, a cot death when he was only ten months old. From what Justine still gathered from family whispers, her mother had had a breakdown over her son's death, and vowed never to have another baby.

When Justine arrived, nearly ten years later, Adelaide had by then perfected her 'non-worrying' mode, and became a splendidly indulgent, rather scatty-headed mother. Justine had been allowed to run wild; the very opposite to the normal smothering reaction to a previous cot death in a family.

This lack of mothering, on top of her father's many absences, meant Justine had grown up with a serious lack of discipline. She'd brilliantly failed most of her exams at school, despite her reports saying she was exceptionally bright. This she had proved, by putting her head down during the last six months of her final year of school—a male classmate had raised her hackles by calling her a blonde bimbo one day—and achieving a surprisingly acceptable pass. Enough to get her onto a degree course at the university not far from where the Montgomerys lived at Lindfield.

She had already spent a delightful three years on the college campus, joining every club it had, partying and having the most fantastic fun. Unfortunately, her frantic social life had resulted in her failing her exams again. In fact, she'd failed her first year two years in a row. At the beginning of this year, when she'd tried to sign up to repeat the first year of her degree course yet again, the dean had suggested she might like to try some other subject. She couldn't think what, and had wangled her way back for a third try, her dazzling smile achieving the dean's agreement with remarkable ease.

Thankfully, she hadn't let him down, and was confident she had sailed through this time. She'd happily finished her last exam this week and was looking forward to moving on to her second year at long last.

'How did you enjoy the party, darling?' her mother asked vaguely as she munched into another chocolate, then turned the page of her book.

'Oh, it was all right, I guess. The same old crowd. Just as well I went in my own car, though, and didn't let Howard pick me up like he wanted to. Truly, he's getting to be a real pain. Just because I've been out with him a couple of times, he thinks he owns me. I was having a perfectly nice time in the pool when he came up behind me, pulled me under the water and tried to take my top off. I was furious, I can tell you. I can't stand being manhandled like that. The way he was carrying on, any-one would think we were sleeping together.'

Adelaide blinked up from her book. 'What was that, dear? Did you say you were sleeping with someone?'

Justine sighed. She could say she was sleeping with the entire male faculty at the university and her mother would not react normally. Truly, one day something would happen that would shock her out of the fog she lived in.

'No, Mum. I said I *wasn't* sleeping with Howard. Howard Barthgate,' she added, when her mother looked vague for a moment.

'Ah, yes. The Barthgate boy. And you're not sleeping with him? That does surprise me, I admit. Such a good-looking boy. But that's the way to re-ally catch them, darling. Don't sleep with them. You couldn't do better, you know. His father has squillions, and Howard's his only son.'

'Mum, I am *not* going to marry Howard Barthgate!'

'Why ever not?'

'Because he's an arrogant, snotty little creep.'

'Is he? I thought he was quite tall when I met him. Oh, well...whatever you think best, dear. Someone else will come along. A girl like you will always have men trailing after her.'

'What do you mean? A girl like me?'

'Oh, you know,' Adelaide said airily. 'Rich. Single. Sexy.'

Justine was surprised by this last adjective. Most mothers would have said pretty, or lovely, or beau-tiful. Justine was not stupid. She saw herself in the mirror every day and she knew she was a good-looking girl.

But sexy? Now she'd never thought of herself as that, mostly because she wasn't all that interested in sex. Never had been really. While all her girl-friends' hormones had been raging for years, she'd sailed along with myriads of boyfriends and dates, but nothing beyond the kissing and minor groping stages.

Actually, it was her aversion to even *minor* grop-ing which stopped her from allowing more. She hated all that heavy breathing stuff. The thought of hot fumbling fingers pawing at her breasts, or a wet sloppy mouth slobbering all over her gave her the heebie-jeebies.

Justine always made it quite clear on the first date that if the boy thought she was going to come across at the end of the night, he could find himself someone else to take out. She had no intention of giving a man sex just because he bought her dinner, or took her to a movie. Only true love, she reasoned loftily, would make such an intimate and yukky act bearable.

Despite this highly unique stance for a nineties girl, Justine still had a great social life, never lack-ing in invitations or escorts. Her life was full of fun, without complication, without the emotional traumas which seemed to come with a sexual re-lationship. All her girlfriends told her tales of woe about their various boyfriends and lovers.

Frankly, Justine thought sex was more trouble than it was worth.

Of course, there *was* an irritating faction within her female friends who thought differently on the subject. Trudy, who lived two streets away from Justine and who'd been her best friend for yonks, was simply mad about men and sex. Only last week she'd assured Justine that one day some hunky guy would come along and sweep her off her feet and into bed before she could blink an eye.

Justine had scoffed at such an unlikely scenario. He'd have to be a man in a million, that was for sure, with a darn lot of sex appeal and know-how. Nothing at all like Howard Barthgate. Dear heaven, she wouldn't be going out with the likes of *him* again!

Dismissing Howard from her mind with her usual slightly ruthless speed, Justine jumped up from her mother's bed. 'I think I'll go make myself some hot chocolate. Want some?'

'No, thank you, darling. Hot chocolate's very fattening,' her mother said with all seriousness as she popped another milk *crème* into her mouth.

Justine kept a straight face with difficulty as she left the room. Truly, the woman was incorrigible. But she was such a dear, with not a mean bone in her body. Justine would not have had her any other way. It was quite wonderful to have a mother who loved you to death but who didn't interfere. Justine liked running her own show. She liked it very much.

Her smile was full of indulgent affection as she skipped down the sweeping central staircase, sliding her hand down the carved mahogany banister on the way and thinking of all the times she'd slid more than her hand down that perfectly polished and thankfully sturdy construction. What a wonderfully carefree and punishment-free childhood she had had! Some people called her spoilt and wilful, but Justine didn't see it that way. She thought she was the luckiest girl in Sydney, and maybe even Australia!

The front doorbell rang just as she jumped off the bottom step into the marble-tiled foyer. She stood there for a moment, startled. Who on earth could be calling at this time of night?

A strange chill invaded Justine as she made her way with uncharacteristic hesitation towards the door.

'Who is it?' she asked through the door, a burst of nerves making her voice sharp.

'The police, ma'am.'

The police! Oh, my God...

She shot back the door chain and wrenched open the door, paling at the sight of the two uniformed officers standing on the front porch. Their serious faces betrayed that their mission was not a pleasant one.

'Mrs Montgomery?' the older officer queried with a frown.

'No. Mum's upstairs in bed. I'm Justine Montgomery, her daughter. What is it? Has something happened to my father?'

When Justine saw their exchanged glances her head began to swim.

Pull yourself together, she ordered herself. Mum is going to need you.

'He...he's dead, isn't he?' she blurted out, a silent scream in her head.

The officer nodded sadly. 'I'm truly sorry, miss.'

'I...I suppose it was a car accident,' she choked

out, thinking how often she'd chided her father for driving too fast.

The two police officers exchanged another, more meaningful glance, and Justine stiffened.

'Er…no, miss. Not a car accident. I'm sorry. I really think that—'

'Tell me, for pity's sake!' she interrupted. 'I need to know the truth!'

The older officer sighed. 'Your father had a fatal coronary in a Kings Cross club where gentlemen go to be…er…entertained.'

Justine rocked back, gripping the front door for support, her eyes wide upon the bearer of this almost unbelievable news.

'Let me get this straight, Sergeant,' she said slowly, her mouth parched. 'Are you saying my father died in a brothel?'

He looked painfully embarrassed and reluctant to repeat his news. 'Um…yes, miss,' he finally admitted. 'That's what I'm saying. Look, I realise this has come as a shock. Unfortunately, there—'

'Who's that at the door, darling?'

The policemen broke off. Justine whirled round.

Adelaide Montgomery was coming down the stairs, sashing her dressing-gown, a frown on her plumply pretty face. 'Is there anything wrong?' she asked worriedly in her little-girl voice.

Justine watched her mother blanch at the sight of the two policemen at the front door, watched as Adelaide's eyes filled with panic and fear. She clutched at the neckline of her robe with both hands as she swayed on unsteady feet. 'Oh, dear God, no! Not Grayson…'

Justine hurried to hold her mother before she fainted, knowing that their lives would never be the same again.

CHAPTER TWO

'A BOARDING house!' her mother exclaimed in horror. 'You want to turn my home into a boarding house? Oh, no, no, no. That would never do, Justine. It's out of the question. Goodness, whatever will my friends think?'

'Who cares what they think?' came Justine's frustrated reply. 'Most of them are just fair-weather friends anyway. How many phone calls or visits have you had from your so-called friends lately?' Justine asked her mother. 'How many invitations? They all came to the funeral, mouthing platitudes of sympathy and support, but as soon as they found out all our money was gone, they dropped us like hot-cakes. It's as though we've suddenly got a brand on our foreheads. *Poor*, it says. *To be given a wide berth.*'

'Oh, Justine, you're imagining things. Why, only yesterday I received an invitation in the mail from Ivy, inviting us both to Felix's fiftieth birthday party this coming Saturday evening.'

Justine refrained from pointing out that that was probably Trudy's doing, Ivy being Trudy's mother. The invitation had been suspiciously late. Yesterday was Wednesday, after all. No doubt Trudy had made a fuss when she'd found out Justine and her mother were not on the guest list for her father's party and insisted her mother ask them.

Justine didn't like Ivy Turrell one bit. She was

an awful snob. Her husband wasn't much better. Felix had made a fortune selling insurance, and only invited people to his home who could be of benefit to him. Naturally, there'd been a time when the well-to-do Montgomerys had always been on the Turrells' guest-list. Not so for much longer, Justine thought ruefully.

'People are giving us a little time to get over our grief,' her mother went on, seeing through her usual rose-coloured glasses. 'We're not *really* poor, and it's only been two months since your father...since he...he...' She slumped down on the side of her unmade bed, her hands twisting together in her lap. 'Since the funeral,' she finished in a strangled tone.

Justine sat down beside her, sliding a comforting arm around her sagging shoulders.

'Mum, we have to face facts. We *are* poor, compared to the people we've been mixing with. Okay, so technically you still own this house and its contents. But we have no income any more. And Daddy died owing nearly half a million dollars.'

'But I don't understand,' her mother wailed. 'Where did all the money go? I inherited a considerable amount from my parents when they passed away. It all came to me. I was their only child.'

'Daddy spent it all, Mum. And in a way, so did we. Neither of us ever asked where he got the money for our generous allowances, did we? We never budgeted, never went out to work ourselves, never questioned our lifestyles of sheer luxury. We just accepted all this as our due,' she finished, waving around at the opulent bedroom, with its silk furnishings and antique furniture.

'But Grayson never liked my asking him questions,' came the tremulous excuse.

Justine patted her mother's hands. 'I know, Mum. I know.'

'He...he used to get angry if I asked him questions.'

Bastard, Justine thought bitterly.

She'd once loved and admired her father, but not any more. She knew the real man now, not the smiling sugar-daddy who'd obviously thought being a husband and father was covered by keeping his wife and daughter's bank accounts topped up. The truth was he'd shamefully neglected his family, relying on his empty charm to keep sweet the women in his life.

Justine was forced to accept now that her father had married her mother for money, never love. Grayson Montgomery's greed had been as prodigious as his lust. One of the worst rumours she'd heard since his death was that he'd taken advantage of several elderly and very wealthy widows who'd consulted him about investments, worming his way into their affections and becoming a beneficiary in their wills—money which he'd subsequently frittered away.

Justine didn't doubt any of it. She only had to look at their own dire financial situation to know the truth about the man. Over the last few years, her father had cashed in every viable asset to bankroll his increasingly expensive lifestyle. His rampant gambling plus regular visits to high-class call girls *had* cost quite a bit. He'd died with no life insurance, a considerable overdraft and a massive personal loan on which the family home had been offered as security. His Jaguar had since been re-possessed, as had her mother's Astra. Only her own Nissan was unencumbered. But even that would have to go. Justine would have to trade it in next week, for a cheaper, smaller model.

'We really don't have *any* money?' her mother asked tearfully.

'None, I'm afraid,' she confessed. 'Daddy's bank is also threatening to sell the house so they can recoup their losses. They will, too.'

Her mother's eyes flooded with tears and her shoulders began to shake. 'But this is my home. My father bought it when he married my mother sixty years ago. I was born here. Brought up here. All my memories are here. I...I couldn't bear to lose this as well.'

Justine could see that. It had been *her* home as well, since her grandparents had passed away. She didn't want to sell the house, but someone had to be practical; someone had to face reality and do something to make ends meet!

Like her mother, Justine had spent her entire life not having to worry about a thing, and it hadn't been easy for her since her father's death. But oddly enough, in adversity Justine had found hidden strengths of character she hadn't realised she possessed. One was a determination not to succumb to self-pity.

'Which is why I'm trying to save it,' she pointed out firmly to her mother. 'The boarding house idea is the only solution. Even so, we're going to have to auction off some of the contents to reduce the loan. I thought I'd start with the things Grandma left me in her will. They're quite valuable, you know.'

Up till today, Justine's mother had simply refused to face what her husband had done, both in life and in death. She'd gone along blithely pretending that everything would come out right in the end if she buried her head in the sand long enough.

Justine watched now as she struggled to accept reality. Unfortunately, her mother's ingrained habit of ignoring unpalatable facts was simply too strong.

Instead of facing their situation, she became stroppy. 'Part with your grandmother's legacy? Absolutely not! I won't hear of it! I...I'll go down to the bank manager myself tomorrow and explain. I'm sure he can wait till we both get jobs and can repay your father's debts.'

Justine could not believe her mother's naïvety! Who on earth was going to employ a fifty-seven-year-old woman who'd never worked in her life? Her own prospects weren't much better!

'Mum, neither of us have skills to offer an employer,' she explained patiently. 'I'd have *some* chance because I'm younger. But nothing fancy. Even if I was lucky enough to get a job in a boutique or a supermarket, my salary would not even touch the sides of the loan repayments. Our only chance is to run a business. We have five spare bedrooms in this house if we share this one. Daddy's study could be made into a bedroom as well, since it has a very comfy convertible sofa. The university is just down the road. We could bring in good money by renting all six rooms to students who want full board.'

'But who would do all the cooking and cleaning? You let Gladys and June go last week.'

'We'll have to do it together, Mum. We can't afford a cook. Or a cleaner. Or a gardener, for that matter.'

'Oh, no, not Tom too,' Adelaide protested.

'Yes, Tom too. We just don't have enough money to pay him. Fact is, Mum, we don't have *any* money left at all. The electricity bill came in this week, and the phone bill is still unpaid since before Christmas. They're threatening to cut us off by the end of the week. We're going to have to sell a few things today to pay those bills and buy some food. Some personal things we don't really need.'

Adelaide's head jerked up, her eyes pained. 'Not my mother's jewellery!'

Justine sighed and stood up. 'It might come to that eventually, but, no, we'll hang on to Grandma's jewellery for a while. We wouldn't get a fraction of what it's worth, anyway. I was thinking of taking a car-load of clothes down to that second-hand clothing store which specialises in designer labels. Just our evening dresses to begin with,' she added when her mother looked appalled. 'I doubt we'll be getting invited to too many dinner parties or fancy dos in future.'

'What about Felix's birthday party?' her mother challenged with a burst of petulance. 'I'll have you know that that invitation said "black tie". What are we going to wear if we sell all our evening clothes?'

'Very well, we'll keep a couple of evening dresses each,' Justine compromised. 'But we'll have to sell some day wear instead. Shoes and bags included. Do you want me to go through your wardrobe and sort something out, or will you?'

Adelaide began shaking her head from side to side. 'This is terrible. Whatever is to become of us?'

'Nothing too terrible, if I can sell my boarding house plan to the man I'm going to see this Friday morning.'

Adelaide glanced up with that blankly childlike expression which made you want to protect her. 'Man? What man?'

'A man in a bank. Not the bank who's threatening to sell us up. One of those merchant banks which specialises in low-interest business loans. Trudy's given me the name of a loans officer there whom she knows personally. It seems he's *simpatico* to damsels in distress.'

Actually, Trudy hadn't put it quite like that.

'Wade has an insatiable appetite for women,' she'd said. 'He'll do anything to get his leg over. I was at a New Year's Eve party the other week and he boasted to me of the loans he'd granted last year in exchange for some slap and tickle. I think he was trying to impress me with his boldness. Didn't do a bad job, either. Given his penchant for female flesh, you'd be sure to qualify for one of his loans.'

'I'm not *that* desperate, Trudy,' Justine had said, shuddering at the thought of giving sex for a loan. That was no better than prostitution!

'No one's suggesting you have to actually come across, Jussie. Of course *I* might, just for the hell of it,' Trudy had added with an impish grin. 'Wade *is* a handsome devil. But I can understand that a girl like you, who's waiting for true love to strike, would not even consider such an outrageous idea!

'So just smile and flirt and flatter the sexy scoundrel. And give him the impression that he'll be amply rewarded if he sanctions your loan. With that face and figure of yours he'll be drooling at the mouth, his brains firmly in his pants as he puts pen to paper.'

'But what will happen when I don't deliver?' Justine had pointed out.

'Oh, he'll be seriously peeved. No doubt about that. But he can hardly go to his boss and complain, can he? Believe me when I say that the head of that particular bank would not take kindly to one of his employees using his position to rubber-stamp loans in exchange for sexual favours. I've met Marcus Osborne. Father's had him over to the house on a couple of occasions. He's a formidable man at the best of times. Ruthlessly ambitious but straight as a die. If he ever finds out what Wade is up to, poor Wade will be out on his ear.'

And well deservedly, Justine had thought at the time. She still did. But she also saw she had no alternative but to keep her appointment with the lecherous Wade or let the house be sold. All Justine's other banking options had finally run out. After a myriad of phone calls, only one other loans officer had consented to see her during the past week, and he'd actually laughed at her idea.

The memory of that laughter hardened Justine's resolve. Come ten o'clock tomorrow morning, she was going to sashay into Wade Hampton's office, ready to do anything to achieve her goal and save her family home. If she had to humiliate herself a little, then she would. If she had to surrender some

of her infernal pride, then too bad. If she had to
beg, then...

No-no, she would *not* beg. That was going too
far.

So was actually sleeping with the man. Good
Lord! The very idea!

'What are you going to wear?' her mother asked.

'What?'

'For your appointment with this man in the bank.
What are you going to wear?'

'I'm not sure. I haven't thought about it yet.'

'Then perhaps you should, before you sell off all
your decent clothes.'

The word 'decent' struck a certain irony with
Justine. Decent was not the look she would be striv-
ing for tomorrow, not if she wanted Wade
Hampton's brains to be addled from the moment
she walked into his office. She needed to wear
something very bright, very tight and very sexy.

A certain lime-green dress popped into her mind.
She'd bought it whilst shopping with Trudy—always a mistake. Trudy was a bad influence at the
best of times. Admittedly, the girl did have an in-
fallible taste for the kind of clothes which made
men sit up and take notice.

This particular dress was made of a double knit
material which clung like Howard Barthgate. It had
a modest enough neckline but was appallingly
short, the tight, straight skirt curving provocatively
around her derrière. Justine had only worn it once,
to lectures late last year. When she'd sat down and
crossed her long tanned legs to one side of her
cramped desk, the poor professor's eyes had nearly
popped out of his head.

Would Wade Hampton's eyes pop out as well?

Justine cringed at the thought, but beggars couldn't be choosers, she'd found out. The rules of her life had changed. She was now playing a new game. It was called survival.

Oddly enough, the thought enthused her. She jumped up from the chair, full of new determination.

'Come on, Mum. Time for us to go downstairs and have a hearty breakfast. We have a lot of work to do today!'

CHAPTER THREE

MARCUS sat at his desk, angrily tapping his gold pen on the leather-inlaid surface, his eyes not properly focused on the paper in his right hand.

He still could not believe the gall of that young man! Not a hint of remorse, or conscience. He hadn't even cared about being dismissed on the spot, without a reference.

Of course he came from a moneyed family, with plenty of the right connections and contacts. He didn't *need* his salary. He hadn't had to work his finger to the bone to make something of himself, to drag himself out of the gutter of abject poverty and succeed against all the odds. Wade Hampton's job as loans officer was really just a fill-in, a way of passing the time till he inherited the Hampton family fortune.

The Wade Hamptons of this world had no idea how the other half lived. They were born with silver spoons in their mouths and grew up without having to toe the line in any way, shape or form.

Even Marcus's diatribe this morning over his lack of moral fibre had not made a single dent in the young man's insolence and arrogance.

When Marcus had been told of Hampton's tendency to approve loans not on the merit of the business venture but on the sexual co-operativeness of the client, he'd seen red. The thought that the reputation of the bank was being besmirched behind his back was like salt rubbed into a raw wound. If there was one thing Marcus valued above all else it was his good name, and the good name of his bank. Yet here was an employee, using his position of power to virtually blackmail women into his bed.

Not that Hampton had seen it that way.

'Blackmail?' he'd scorned when this accusation had been thrown at him. 'I don't have to blackmail women to go to bed with me. Not the second time, anyway,' he'd smirked. 'There's nothing wrong with what I did. Everyone was happy. Me. The ladies. And your stupid old bank. Not one of my loans has ever been foreclosed. It's only stuffed shirts like you who think combining business with pleasure is a crime. God, just look at you. You dress like an undertaker. And you act like my grandfather. I'll bet you haven't been to bed with a bird in donkey's years.

'But that's *your* problem. As are my appointments for today,' he'd declared as he whirled and strode for the door. 'I'm outta here!'

A good fifteen minutes had passed since Hampton's departure, during which time Marcus had instructed his secretary to inform Personnel of the situation, then get him a computer printout of the loans officer's appointments for that Friday, all of which had been done with her usual efficiency.

It was Marcus who was not operating with *his* usual efficiency. The appointment list had been in his hands for a full five minutes, yet he hadn't been able to concentrate on the names. Hampton's comment about his sex life—or lack of it—still rankled.

How long *had* it been since he'd been to bed with a woman?

Too damned long, came the testy realisation.

Clenching his teeth, Marcus dragged his attention back to the paper in his hands, his eyes widening, then narrowing when he spied the first name on the list.

Hampton's ten o'clock appointment—his first for the day—was none other than Miss Justine Montgomery!

Marcus's surprise was only exceeded by his curiosity. What on earth was the wealthy Miss Montgomery doing coming to *his* bank for a loan? She must know they specialised in business loans. What use would she have for such a loan?

Did she fancy herself going into some small business to pass her idle hours away till she landed herself a rich husband? An art gallery perhaps? Or a fashion boutique? A trendy coffee shop?

Marcus could only guess. There was one way of finding out for certain, he supposed. Take the appointment himself and ask.

The thought of seeing Miss Montgomery again— and in a position where he had the upper hand— held an insidious attraction. Marcus began to appreciate what Hampton had found so appealing about his job. To have a woman—especially an incredibly beautiful young woman—beholden to you. To have it in your power to give her something *she* wanted in exchange for something *you* wanted...

Marcus's pulse rate quickened as he contemplated such a corrupting scenario. Justine Montgomery had lived on in his memory since that warm November night two months before, when he'd surreptitiously watched her almost naked body emerge from that pool. He still recalled every inch of her physical perfection, from her impossibly long legs to her tight little bottom to her lushly nubile breasts.

How would you like to go to bed with *her*? the devil whispered in his ear.

He stood up abruptly, took a fob watch from a pocket in his waistcoat and checked the time. Five to ten. He had two options. He could have Miss Montgomery's appointment rescheduled to a later date with another loans officer. Or he could go downstairs to Loans and see her himself.

His experience-honed instinct for avoiding trouble warned him to have her rescheduled, but when he glanced up and glimpsed his reflection in the wide semicircular window which wrapped around behind his desk, Hampton's insults once again jumped into his mind.

He glared hard at the man glaring back, the pompously dressed stuffed shirt who believed combining business with pleasure was a crime...

His reflection faded from his conscious mind as another vision took over, that of Justine Montgomery's lovely yet startled face as he laid out the terms for her getting a loan. His mouth dried as he imagined the moment when he first drew her into his arms. He could actually feel her initial reluctance, feel the fluttering of her heart against his chest.

Till he kissed her.

After that there was no more resistance, only the most delicious surrender as she melted against him...

Marcus gritted his teeth as the painful hardening in his trousers brought him back to reality. He knew

he would never do such a disgusting thing as blackmail her into his bed. But he couldn't stop thinking
about it. There was something darkly compelling
about the idea of having Justine Montgomery in his
sexual power.

Common sense and professionalism demanded
he steer well clear of the girl, now that his carnal
desires were engaged.

But both were poor arguments against the excitement which beckoned just one floor down.

Not that he was going to try to coerce or corrupt
the girl, Marcus reassured himself as he stuffed the
fob watch back into its pocket and strode from the
room. Nothing—not even the most desirable female
in the world—would induce him to stoop to such
low behaviour.

The possibility that the incredibly desirable
Justine Montgomery might try to coerce or corrupt
him had yet to occur to Marcus Osborne.

Justine glanced at her watch as she stepped from
the lift. Five to ten.

Scooping in a steadying breath, she straightened
her shoulders and walked with her head held high
to the large reception desk straight ahead. Not normally a nervous girl, she had to admit to wild flut-
terings in her stomach that morning. It would have
been so easy to turn and flee. But fleeing was out
of the question. Anyone with a brain in their heads
could see her mother might have another breakdown if she lost her home on top of everything else.
Justine had listened to the poor love cry herself to
sleep last night, the awful sounds reaffirming her

determination to get this darned loan if it was the last thing she did.

The pretty brunette behind the desk stopped tapping on her PC and glanced up as Justine approached.

'May I help you?' she asked politely.

'I'm Justine Montgomery. I have a ten o'clock appointment with Mr Hampton.'

'Oh, yes, Miss Montgomery. Wade's away from his desk at the moment, but I know he's somewhere in the building. I'm sure he'll be with you in a moment. I'll take you along to his office and you can wait for him there.'

Mr Hampton's office was minute, more of a walled cubicle than a real office. Justine settled herself in the single chair which faced the less than impressive desk to await the loans officer's arrival. She recrossed her legs several times, none of the positions finding favour. Her long stockingless legs still felt awfully overexposed. She tried sitting with her knees pressed primly together but knew that looked ridiculous.

Steeling her nerves, she dropped the handbag she'd been clutching in her lap down by the legs of the chair and crossed her legs one last time, steadfastly ignoring the way the skirt rode up dangerously high. Another glance at her watch told her it was one minute past ten.

Two minutes later, she heard firm footsteps coming down the tiled corridor. She twisted her head round just as a man strode in and closed the door behind him.

Justine blinked, trying not to look as taken aback

as she was. But surely this couldn't be Wade Hampton!

For starters, Justine had been expecting someone much younger, not a man in his mid-thirties! Trudy's taste in men usually ran to the toy-boy type, with pretty-boy looks, longish hair and wickedly dancing eyes, trendy dressers who smiled at the drop of a hat and oozed a type of cheeky sex appeal.

Justine could not help but stare as *this* man stalked into the room, his face seemingly set in concrete. No smile of greeting softened that hard mouth, or those deeply set black eyes.

Admittedly he *was* a handsome devil, with a strikingly sculptured face, a sensually shaped mouth and deeply set dark eyes which sent shivers down her spine. But that black pin-striped suit, though impressively tailored, was anything but trendy, and his ruthlessly cut black hair was plastered back like Michael Douglas in that movie *Wall Street*.

He looked about as warm and as approachable as a Kremlin advisor on nuclear waste, hardly the type to be susceptible to flirting or flattery, *or* a short, tight lime-green dress!

'Good morning, Miss Montgomery,' he said brusquely, his handsome face coldly unreadable. 'Sorry to keep you waiting.'

He moved around behind his desk and sat down, his dark eyes immediately dropping to scan the application form he'd carried in with him. It was a full minute before he glanced up at her.

'So how may I help you, Miss Montgomery?' he asked quite curtly.

The dean had spoken to her in a similarly cool

fashion when she'd gone to him for permission to repeat the year. Yet he'd warmed to her soon enough once she smiled at him.

Justine found that same smile, flashing it for all its worth at the loans officer. 'I have a business proposition to put to your bank, Mr Hampton. I think it's a very good proposition and one which would benefit both of us.'

Marcus just sat there for a long moment, frozen to the chair.

She thought he was Wade Hampton.

Understandable, considering. He hadn't enlightened her otherwise, although he'd meant to, before the sight of those incredible legs had distracted him.

His eyes washed over her more thoroughly, taking in the provocative little green dress, the highly glossed mouth, the beautiful but overbright eyes. She was either nervous, or excited. Or both.

Marcus's suspicions were instantly aroused. Did Miss Montgomery know of Wade Hampton's reputation for being a loans officer of easy virtue? Had she come here today armed with that knowledge, ready and willing to barter her delectable young body in exchange for a business loan of some kind? Was that what she meant when she said her proposition could benefit both of them?

The possibility gave a serious push to his already teetering conscience. But, dear God, she was breathtakingly beautiful, even more when she smiled.

Beautiful but bad, came the silent reminder.

Well, he didn't know that for sure, did he? Not yet. And, if he were honest, he wouldn't mind so much if she was bad. Not now, at this very moment, with his loins aching. Who knew what she might do if she'd come here ready and willing to be *really* bad? The various scenarios such thinking evoked did little for his already painful arousal.

Marcus stared at the object of his darkest desires for a few more moments before deciding not to tell her who he was. He settled back as best he could in Hampton's narrow chair and waited for her to put her foot further into her pretty mouth.

'Is that so?' he said, steepling his fingers across his chest and trying not to eat her up too much with his eyes. But it was difficult not to wonder just how far she would go if he dangled the right carrot in front of those full sensual lips of hers.

He had to clear his throat before going on, not to mention his mind. Damn, but the girl was a temptation all right. If the devil wanted to send someone to corrupt him, he could not have chosen anyone more perfect.

'Perhaps if you could outline your proposition to me,' he said, 'I would be better able to judge its benefit to both of us.'

Justine heard the sardonic edge in his voice, and hesitated. He knew—knew she was going to flirt with him, knew she was going to subtly offer herself as part of the loan package. He was sitting there, waiting like a big black spider for her to walk into his web.

Pride demanded she jump up straight away and stalk out of there.

But pride was not going to get her a loan. It would be cold comfort when she went home and explained to her mother that the house would have to be sold. Pride would not be of much value to Justine when they carted her mother off to some sanitarium or other.

Practicality won over pride. As did pragmatism. Who cared what he thought of her? The man was a creep. A user and abuser of women.

Well, it's *you* who's going to be used this time, buster, Justine thought. She flashed another winning smile at him, then launched into an explanation of her present financial situation.

Hampton frowned when she told him of her father's death and subsequent debts, the frown deepening when she revealed the other bank's intention to sell up the house and recoup their losses.

'Can they do that?' she asked abruptly.

'They're within their legal rights. Will the value of the house cover the entire debt?'

'Oh, easily. It's worth a million at least.'

'Mmm.'

'My mother doesn't want to sell, Mr Hampton. And neither do I. If you could see your way clear to taking over the loan at business rates and giving me a little time, I have a plan whereby I'm sure I can repay the entire loan.'

His dark eyebrows arched. 'Really. Perhaps you'd better tell me about this plan.'

'I'd be glad to. Firstly, I could substantially reduce the loan within a few short weeks by auctioning off some the house's contents.'

'I see. And how much do you think you could raise this way?'

'I'm sure I could cut the loan down to two hundred thousand dollars.'

'How did you plan on repaying the final two hundred thousand?'

'In the normal way, with monthly repayments.'

'You'd still be looking at repayments of two thousand dollars a month. Where will the money come from to make those repayments, Miss Montgomery?'

The logical question led Justine into an outline of her boarding house project. To give Hampton credit, he listened politely, asking her relevant questions about how much she thought she would get for each room, and what her weekly profit might be. Clearly he didn't just rubber-stamp any old loan, regardless of the fringe benefits.

'I'm sorry, Miss Montgomery,' he said at last. 'I'm afraid we can't help you. Your plan just *isn't* financially feasible. It has too many variables. I really think it would be in your best interests for you and your mother to sell the house and buy something smaller with what money is left over.'

'But I don't *want* to live in anything smaller,' Justine suddenly snapped, shock and nerves getting the better of her.

One of those straight black brows arched.

Justine gritted her teeth. She should be simpering at him, not snapping. Flirting, not flaring up. God, but it was hard to grovel.

'My mother hasn't been well,' she tried explaining. 'She's still grieving for my father and it would break her heart to lose her home. Please,' she pleaded, looking straight into his eyes and breaking her vow not to beg. 'I know I can make a success of this.'

For a moment she was sure she had him—and

without having to humiliate herself too much. But then he wrenched his eyes away, snapping forward on his chair.

'I am not unsympathetic to your position, Miss Montgomery,' he said, looking back at her. 'If you had a steady job to back up your boarding house plan, I would have no hesitation in sanctioning this loan. But you've listed your occupation as a university student. What exactly are you studying?'

'I've been doing a degree in Leisure Studies.'

'Leisure Studies,' he repeated drily.

Justine supposed it did sound a bit empty.

'I'm specialising in Tourism Management,' she elaborated. 'It's much more complicated than it sounds. And should lead to a well-paid job. Eventually.'

'And how long have you to go?'

'I've...um...just finished my first year.'

'Only your first year? Yet your application form says you're twenty-one—twenty-two next month. What did you do when you left school? Travel?'

'No. I...er...failed my first year a couple of times.'

'I see,' was his dry remark.

'No, you don't,' she defended sharply. 'I'm not dumb, Mr Hampton. I just didn't apply myself properly. I was too busy having fun. But I can do anything, once I apply myself.'

'Anything, Miss Montgomery?' he mocked.

Justine bristled. 'Well, almost anything,' she snapped. 'I doubt I could be a brain surgeon. But running a boarding house shouldn't be beyond me. My mother would help.'

'I thought you said your mother hadn't been well.'

'She's not physically sick. It's more of an emotional problem, one which would be solved if she could stay in her home.'

Justine waited for him to say something but he didn't. My God, for a supposedly inveterate womaniser, he wasn't making this easy for her. Maybe he enjoyed watching women grovel. Maybe he got a kick out of reducing them to pathetic pawns in his sick little power game.

She swallowed, pushed the remnants of her pride to the back of her mind, then took the plunge. 'I'll try to get a job, Mr Hampton. I will do anything you want. *Anything,*' she repeated, making strong eye contact and promising him all sort of things with her eyes and her softly parted lips.

Once again he said nothing, although he did stare at those lips. Justine's stomach tightened, her mouth drying in the face of his unnerving silence.

'If you give me this loan, Mr Hampton,' she added shakily, 'you will have my undying gratitude.'

'But I don't *want* your gratitude, Miss Montgomery,' he said quite coldly.

Justine felt her face flame into embarrassed heat as those hard black eyes looked her over. Never before had she felt so small, or so irritatingly lacking in confidence. Confusion reigned supreme. Her heart was racing, her stomach turning over and over.

'Then what *is* it you want?' she threw at him in her fluster.

Let *him* be the one to belittle himself now,

Justine thought raggedly. Let him say it out loud, show the world what sort of man he *really* was, not this coolly controlled customer who looked as if he'd never put a foot wrong in his life!

Then she was going to get up and walk out. She might even report him to his boss. What was his name? Osborne. Marcus Osborne. Yes, she'd go and tell Mr Marcus Osborne the kind of man he had in his employ!

'I want you to go home and convince your mother to sell the house,' he shocked her by saying in a harsh tone. 'Then I want you to go and get yourself a proper job. But, most of all, I want you to stop playing provocative and potentially dangerous games. You think I don't know what you were getting at just now, Miss Montgomery? You're not the first beautiful young woman to tempt me. And I dare say you won't be the last!

'There is no quick and easy way in life, Justine,' he lectured on while her mouth dropped open. 'Not if you're a decent human being with values and standards. Don't go down your father's path. You're far too young and far too beautiful to sell yourself so cheaply.'

Justine went bright, bright red. Embarrassed beyond belief, she grabbed her bag and jumped to her feet. 'I don't know what you're talking about. If you don't want to give me the loan, then just say so. There's no need to insult me.'

'Very well. I'm not going to give you the loan.'

'Fine. Then I'll get the money some other way!'

Marcus watched her whirl round and flounce out. He almost called her back, almost told her that he'd changed his mind and the loan was hers.

But of course that was impossible now. He'd done his dash in more ways than one. But by God, there'd been a moment there, a deliciously dark moment, when he'd almost taken her up on her none too subtle offer.

Just think, Marcus, he mocked himself. You could have been taking her out tonight if you'd played your cards right. Taking her out, then taking her back home, to bed, maybe for the whole weekend.

And what did you do?

You wimped out.

He muttered an expletive under his breath.

Now all he had to look forward to this weekend was Felix's fiftieth birthday party.

He hated parties these days, but sometimes he just had to get out of the house—that bloody awful house which he'd bought for Stephany and which she'd graced for less than twelve months. He'd sell the darned thing if it wasn't such a good investment.

Marcus scowled at himself anew. Is that all you think about, Marcus? Good investments? Returns on your money? There's more to life than money, you know.

Or so his beloved wife had thrown at him the day he'd thrown her out.

Which was ironic, because she'd certainly needed plenty of cold hard cash to support the lifestyle she'd grown accustomed to. Women like her always did.

His mind turned to Justine Montgomery once more. He'd felt sorry for her there for a while. Her father might have been a rotter but he'd still been her father. It must have been pretty terrible to have him not only die, but to die in debt and disgrace.

Any sympathy had been dashed, however, when she'd said she had no intention of moving to a smaller house. Not for girls like her a simpler life, or a simpler house. Heaven forbid!

Her boarding house plan was laughable. Did she have any idea how much work would be involved in running such an operation? Did she think she could manage to do it on the side whilst continuing her degree in Leisure Studies?

Her choice of degree was deliciously ironic as well. Girls like Justine Montgomery made an art form of 'leisure'. They didn't have to study the subject. It came naturally to them. As did bartering their bodies for betterment of their circumstances, although mostly it was an advantageous marriage on their minds, not a miserable loan.

Why, you're a cynic, Marcus, came the none too surprising self-realisation. Not to mention a self-righteous holier-than-thou bore. Even with her tarnished soul, Justine Montgomery has more life and fun in her little finger than you have in your whole body.

'Oh, shut up!' he growled, and got to his feet. 'I don't need this.'

Too right, that merciless inner voice shot back. What you need is some decent sex!

CHAPTER FOUR

'MUM, you're not ready!' Justine exclaimed on going into her mother's room and finding her sitting on the side of the bed, still in her bathrobe, her hair in rollers. Yet it was right on eight-thirty, the time they'd agreed to leave for Felix's party.

Adelaide gave her daughter a wan little smile. 'I've decided not to go, darling. But *you* go. Goodness, but don't you look gorgeous? Red is definitely your colour. And I love your hair up like that. You look so sophisticated.'

Justine ignored the barrage of compliments, seeing them for what they were: her mother's way of deflecting her attention from the reality of the situation, which was that she was slumped down on her still unmade bed, trying to be bright and brave when in fact her eyes were once again shimmering with tears. She'd cried on and off since Justine had told her yesterday the house would probably have to be sold. Cried and just sat around, looking defeated and depressed.

Justine had hoped the party tonight might buck her up. She hated seeing her mother like this, so unlike her usual happy if scatty self.

'Oh, no, you don't, Mum,' Justine said, knowing firmness was sometimes the best way with her mother. 'I'm not going by myself.' She walked over to where a beaded black crêpe gown was draped over the gold velvet chair in the corner. 'Is this the dress you're going to wear? Come on, let's get it on you and then I'll help you with you hair. It won't matter if we're late. Parties never get going till well after nine anyway.'

'I can't wear that dress,' Adelaide said bleakly.

'Why not?'

'It doesn't fit me.'

'Doesn't fit you,' Justine repeated, clenching her teeth down hard in her jaw. They must have taken thirty evening gowns of her mother's down to the second-hand shop yesterday, and one of the two dresses her mother had chosen to keep didn't fit her. Truly, 'vague' did not begin to describe her sometimes!

'Then what about the other dress? Where is it?'

'It doesn't fit me either. Neither of the dresses I kept fit me,' her mother confessed on a strangled sob. 'I didn't realise how much weight I'd put on since your father's funeral. I...I always eat when I'm unhappy. I was so pretty and slim when Grayson married me. He loved me back then; I'm sure he did. But after my baby boy died, I started to eat and I...I... Oh, God, it's no wonder your father never wanted to come home. It's all my fault he went with other women. Everything's all my fault!'

Justine's heart felt as if it was breaking as she watched her mother dissolve into sobs. She rushed over to her, gathering her close, hugging her fiercely. 'Don't cry, Mum,' she choked out. 'Please don't cry. Nothing's your fault. Nothing! Daddy didn't deserve you. He wasn't a very nice man. In fact, he was quite wicked. We're well rid of him. But you've still got me. We're going to make it together, Mum, don't you worry,' she went on, fired up with renewed resolve. 'I haven't given up yet on getting that loan.'

Her mother glanced up at her through soggy lashes. 'You haven't?'

'Not by a long shot! There are other banks, aren't there? Other establishments which lend money? Felix's party will be full of influential people to-night, moneyed men with plenty of contacts. I'll keep my eyes and ears open and who knows? I bet I have some good news for you by the time I come home.'

Justine leant over and swept a handful of tissues from the box beside the bed. 'Now, dry your eyes, Mum. And don't give up hope. Your daughter has just begun to fight!'

Justine's newly found optimism wavered during the short drive to the Turrells' place. It was all very well to spout positive aspirations, quite another to put them into action. Giving her mother false hopes might have done the trick for one night, but what would happen in the morning, when she *didn't* have any good news?

Justine sighed, then sighed again when she turned into the leafy street which housed the Turrell mansion. It was lined with cars, not a spare parking spot in sight.

Negotiating a U-turn, Justine finally found a place to park in the adjoining street, the lengthy walk back bringing her attention to the tightness of her skirt. Keeping this little red number had been a bad choice, really. It wasn't at all versatile and could only be worn on really warm evenings.

She'd spotted it in the window of a very exclusive boutique back at the beginning of spring, the red colour attracting her attention. She always kept an eye out for a red dress in the months leading up to Christmas, because she liked to wear red at the big Christmas party her mother threw every year.

Naturally, this year there hadn't been any Christmas party. Justine had found the dress when she'd gone through her wardrobe, and just couldn't bring herself to sell it for a fraction of its value, unworn. It had cost a small fortune, being an original design made from raw silk.

Still, she now regretted keeping it. She should have kept her little black crêpe number along with the black velvet. People didn't remember black, whereas they could see her coming in this red for miles. Dumb choice, Justine. Dumb, dumb, dumb!

By the time she'd manoeuvred her way up the steep front steps in her high heels and rung the front doorbell, Justine was wishing she'd stayed home with her mother.

Trudy opened the door, scowling at the sight of the latecomer. 'So *there* you are! I was beginning to think you weren't coming. And after I'd twisted Mother's arm to get you an invite. Where's your mum?'

'She didn't feel up to it. A headache.'

'Oh, well, perhaps it's for the best.'

Justine bristled. 'How do you see that?'

'Oh, you know my mother, Jussie. She's not the most tactful woman in the world. She'd probably put her big foot in her mouth and say something to offend your mum. She's not sweet-natured like me, darling. She's a natural bitch.'

Justine had to smile. 'You *are* sweet-natured, Trudy. I sometimes wonder if Ivy's your mother.'

Trudy grinned and drew her friend inside, shutting the door behind her. 'Do you think I might be adopted?' she quipped.

'Could be.'

'What a cheery thought! Come on, let's go upstairs and install your purse in my room, then we'll go get a drink and toast the success of plan B for you tonight. At least you're dressed for it,' she added cryptically, her finely plucked eyebrows waggling at Justine's red dress.

Trudy set off up the sweeping staircase at speed, Justine struggling to keep up. 'Plan B? What on earth's plan B?'

'Finding you a rich hubbie. After all, plan A at the bank obviously didn't work.'

'How do you know it didn't?'

'Aside from my lack of faith in your vamping abilities?' came Trudy's dry remark. 'One look at your face on the doorstep, darling, and I knew the truth. You *do* wear your heart on your sleeve sometimes. Not that that dress has sleeves. Actually, it doesn't have much of anything, does it?' she added with a wry sidewards glance. 'So what happened? Did you chicken out yesterday?'

'Not at all. I did everything you told me to do, bar throw myself naked across his desk. I even wore my lime-green dress. He still knocked me back.'

'*Wade* knocked you back?' Trudy was incredulous.

'He not only knocked me back, he gave me a lecture on moral values.'

'I don't believe it!'

'Well, he did.'

They'd reached Trudy's bedroom, which was as large and luxurious as the rest of the house. Frankly, the Turrell mansion made the Montgomery residence look like a miner's cabin by comparison.

Trudy took Justine's purse and put it down on her white-glossed dressing-table, then proceeded to primp and preen in the gilt-framed mirror above it. Trudy was not traditionally beautiful, but she was very attractive, with a voluptuous figure and big brown eyes.

'Maybe someone at the bank was finally on to him,' Trudy mused as she replenished her lipstick and sprayed some perfume down her considerable cleavage. 'Maybe he had to put on a show.'

'Maybe. I can only tell you it was ghastly. I wanted the floor to open and swallow me up, I can tell you.'

'Gosh, how awful for you. Poor Jussie.' Trudy still looked more amused than sympathetic. 'As soon as I've finished here, we'll go and get some champers. Then we'll put plan B into action. I presume Howard Barthgate is out?'

'Yuk!'

'Pity. He fancies you like mad.'

'Not since I lost all my money, he doesn't! I haven't heard from him once. Look, I have no intention of adopting your plan B, Trudy Turrell. Even if I did, I wouldn't let *you* pick me any candidates. From your description of Wade, I at least expected him to ooze sex appeal and charm, but he was as cold as a cucumber sandwich.'

'He must have been putting on an act.'

'I don't know about that. If he was, then he's a damned good actor.'

'You have to admit he's a good-looking devil, though.'

'Yes, I suppose so. Those dark eyes of his certainly sent shivers up and down my spine.'

'Really? Well, that's a first with you, isn't it? From what you've told me, men usually leave *you* pretty cold. Maybe you've met your match at long last.'

'Don't be silly!' Justine refuted. 'I despise men like Wade Hampton.' Which she did. Yet, in truth, she hadn't been able to get the man out of her mind, though her skin still crawled with embarrassment whenever her thoughts turned to him.

'Right, I'm ready,' Trudy said, spinning round and linking arms with Justine. 'Let's go downstairs and knock 'em dead!'

Trudy led Justine down the sweeping staircase and along the wide, tiled hallway to the huge living room, where the bulk of the party-goers had gathered. Justine glanced around, noting that most of the people inside were middle-aged, the younger ones having gravitated out to the pool area on the terrace.

Her gaze landed on Trudy's mother, who looked like mutton dressed up as lamb in a blue satin strapless dress. She had that plastic smile on her overpainted face and was gazing in rapt attention up at a man who had his back turned towards Justine. Not Felix. This man was taller, with black hair and broad shoulders.

Suddenly he turned side-on, and Justine nearly died.

'Oh, my God!' she gasped. 'Why didn't you tell me he was here?'

'Who?'

'Wade Hampton, that's who!'

'Wade? Here? I don't think so. He wasn't invited.'

'Well, he must have come with someone else, because I can see him right over there as clear as a bell.'

'Where?'

'Over there, talking to your mother.'

'Are you crazy? That's not Wade! That's Marcus Osborne!'

'What?'

The two girls stared at each other for a long moment before the penny dropped for both of them. Justine was horrified while Trudy laughed.

'Dear God, Jussie,' she giggled. 'How did you manage to mistake Marcus Osborne for Wade? Oh, heavens, that's funny. No wonder he gave you a lecture when you came on to him. Oh, I wish I'd been a fly on the wall yesterday! What a riot!'

'I don't think it's funny at all!' Justine fumed, glaring over at the man who'd deceived her not accidentally but quite deliberately. He'd known darned well she'd thought he was Wade Hampton when he'd come into Wade's office and sat down at Wade's desk.

But had he informed her of her mistake? Not on your nelly! He'd waited for her to make a none too subtle pass, then cut her down to size. Clearly he'd heard of Wade's little peccadillos and decided to sit in on the action for himself for once.

'I guess we can cross Marcus Osborne off the list

for plan B as well,' Trudy mocked by her side. 'I think you might have blotted your copybook with him a tad, which is a pity. He's filthy rich, and conveniently divorced. You sort of fancied him too, didn't you?'

Trudy nudged a momentarily speechless Justine in the ribs. 'Maybe you're into older men, Jussie. Maybe that's why none of the boys you've gone out with ever got past first base. You probably need a more mature male to turn you on—some cold-blooded brooding banker with loads of unleashed passion. Recognise the description? By golly, our cold-blooded brooding banker *does* look smashing in that tux. I didn't realise how handsome Marcus was till this moment.'

'Handsome is as handsome does,' Justine muttered darkly. 'As for his turning me on, the Arctic will melt before he turns *me* on.'

Trudy was right, though. That dinner jacket and dazzling white dress shirt *did* suit him, much more so than the funereal pin-striped number he'd worn the previous day. Suddenly he looked younger, and sleeker, and, yes, sexier, if you went for the coolly sophisticated type. Which she didn't!

Hatred fizzed and bubbled along her veins as she glared at him.

'You're blushing, Jussie,' Trudy teased.

'No, I'm not. It's my blood pressure boiling. Now, if you'll excuse me, I have something to say to our banking friend. Something which won't wait!'

Justine's blue eyes narrowed as she set off across the room. If Marcus Osborne thought he could get away with treating her in such a shabby fashion, then he could think again!

CHAPTER FIVE

MARCUS felt the hairs on the back of his neck stand on end. Ivy was prattling on about how lovely it was to see him, and how he really should get out more, but his mind was no longer on his hostess. He could see something out of the corner of his eye, someone in red.

He turned his head ever so slightly, then froze. Dear God, it was Justine Montgomery, marching towards him, her furious face telling it all. Clearly someone had told her his true identity, and she was intent on having it out with him.

Anger did become her, he thought ruefully. As did movement. Her obviously braless breasts undulated beneath the provocative little red dress she was wearing, their untettered curves held precariously in place by the halter-necked style. His flesh stirred uncomfortably, and he was thankful to be wearing a jacket.

'I'd like to talk to you,' she snapped as she ground to a halt beside him.

'Justine, *really*!' Ivy protested haughtily. 'It's very rude to interrupt.'

'And it's very rude to pretend to be someone you're not!' she declared, glowering up at the object of her fury.

Whilst Marcus could admire her courage, he had no intention of letting the girl defame him in public.

'Good evening, Miss Montgomery,' he said with

51

cool politeness. 'It's very nice to see you again. Yes, I agree with you. Such pretence *is* reprehensible, but the fact is I didn't realise till after you left the bank yesterday that you thought I was Mr Hampton during our meeting. A most regrettable occurrence and one I must apologise for.

'Ivy, my dear,' he said, addressing himself to his hostess, 'I have some banking business to discuss with Miss Montgomery. Do you have somewhere we could talk privately for a few minutes?'

He congratulated himself on successfully disarming his adversary, at least long enough to shepherd her away from prying eyes and flapping ears. But no sooner had a curious Ivy left them in Felix's study than those big and very beautiful blue eyes narrowed again.

'That was a lie!' she accused. 'You knew darned well I thought you were Wade Hampton yesterday, didn't you?'

'Not to begin with,' he hedged.

'Soon enough!'

'Not till it was too awkward to tell you the truth.'

'Oh, codswallop! You knew what I was going to do and you deliberately set out to trap me. What I'd like to know is why, Mr Osborne? Did you enjoy watching me make a fool of myself? Did you get a thrill out of my belittling myself in front of you?'

What could he say?

'Don't be ridiculous. Of course not.'

'I don't believe you,' she raged on. 'But no matter. I just wanted you to know that I had no intention of delivering anything I might have appeared to promise. Not for Wade Hampton or for you.

Especially not for you, Mr Osborne. Wild horses wouldn't get me into bed with you!'

'Is that so?'

'Yes, that's so. I don't go to bed with men for money. And I especially don't go to bed with men who have ice in their veins instead of blood!'

'I'll keep that in mind, Miss Montgomery,' he said coldly. 'But let's not get into a slanging match. Believe me when I say I didn't deliberately set out to trap you yesterday. Mr Hampton's misuse of his position had just reached my ears and I was... upset.'

'Upset?' she sneered at him. 'Men like you don't get upset! They have their egos put out, that's all. You humiliated me! And you *enjoyed* humiliating me!'

Marcus stiffened, indignation obliterating any guilt he was feeling. Who was *she* to judge him? He only had *her* word for it that she hadn't been going to deliver. Frankly, he didn't believe that for a moment. She was like the thief who wasn't sorry for what he'd done but was darned sorry he'd been caught.

What really irked Marcus most was that she wasn't in any dire financial situation which might have warranted such extreme action. He might have been sympathetic if she'd been in real need, if she and her mother were down to their last dollar. But both of them could live quite comfortably on the left-overs if they sold the house and repaid that debt.

But, no, they had to have it all. The high-class home to go with the high-class lifestyle. The final nail in Miss Montgomery's coffin was that she was here tonight, swanning around in a dress worth more than a working-class girl could spend on her wardrobe in a year!

Marcus recognised designer labels when he saw them. That little scrap of red silk she was almost wearing had not been bought off the rack. It had big dollars written all over it, not to mention sex.

Marcus couldn't keep his eyes off the way it hugged her perfect figure, displaying everything she had to offer a man. Justine Montgomery was no misunderstood innocent. She was a clever, calculating, conniving creature, who wanted what she wanted and was frustrated at being thwarted.

'I didn't humiliate you,' he pointed out frostily. 'You humiliated yourself.'

Justine glared at him and thought she had never hated a man so much. Her heart was hammering wildly in her chest. She was actually quivering from head to foot. Yet *he* was standing before her like a marble statue, his face a stony mask, his eyes as hard as ebony. His cold indifference to her distress forced her to regroup and control her temper. In a fashion.

'You're right,' she admitted shakily. 'I did. But at least I had a good reason. What's *your* excuse?'

'*My* excuse?' he said in an almost startled fashion.

'You don't have one, do you? Men like you don't think you need one. You're above explanations, and excuses, and apologies. Yesterday you gave me a lecture on moral values. But I wonder, Mr Osborne, if your own life would bear too close an inspection. Are you as pure as the driven snow? When was the last time you slept with a woman for reasons other than true love? When was the last time you made a successful investment using information you gleaned from an inside source?'

Justine was taken aback when an angry red slashed across his cheekbones. 'I have never done any such thing!'

'What?'

'Been guilty of insider trading. As for sleeping with women for reasons other than true love... true love is a rare commodity these days, Miss Montgomery. However, I do try to choose bed-partners I both like and respect.'

'Which should narrow prospective candidates down considerably, I would imagine,' she shot back, piqued by the fact he neither liked nor respected *her*.

'I don't usually have any trouble.'

'With such impossibly high standards?'

He glared at her and she quaked a little in her high heels. Goodness, but he *was* a formidable man. Trudy had been right there. But oh, so self-righteous!

'Have you quite finished, Miss Montgomery?'

'No, I damned well haven't! You think you're so superior, don't you? Sitting up there behind your undoubtedly big desk in that big bank of yours and deciding who'll be bailed out and who won't. You no doubt sacked Wade Hampton for what he'd been up to, but you weren't any better yesterday. Apart from your vile deception, you didn't give me a fair hearing. You didn't listen to my proposition with an open mind. Your ugly preconceptions blinded you to what was actually a legitimate business proposition.'

'Come now, Miss Montgomery, do you honestly expect me to feel confident that someone like you could run a boarding house of that size?'

'Someone like me? What do you mean, someone like me?' Justine suddenly saw red. 'Oh, I get it! You think I'm useless. Some spoilt, lazy little rich bitch who's never done a proper day's work in her life.'

'*You* said that. I didn't.'

'But you *think* it,' she snapped.

'If the cap fits, Miss Montgomery...'

Justine was genuinely taken aback. She opened her mouth to tear some more strips off him, then closed it again. She supposed he had a point. She *was* a spoilt little rich bitch. And she *hadn't* done a proper day's work in her life. Not for her living, anyway. But she wasn't useless. And she certainly wasn't lazy.

Suddenly it was important for her to prove that to this man who thought he knew it all! Her chin lifted and she set determined eyes on him.

'I challenge you to give me a chance to prove you wrong, Mr Osborne. Give me that loan and give me six months. If I don't meet my repayments during that time then I'll sell up the house and call it quits. Six months, Mr Osborne,' she repeated. 'It's not much to ask for. As I mentioned before, the house is worth over a million. You've got nothing to lose.'

'You really think so?' he said archly.

'Yes, I do. Look, I promised myself once I'd do anything for this loan but beg. And I won't beg now. But if you don't give me that loan, Mr Osborne, I hope you go to hell and burn there for all eternity!'

He laughed. He actually laughed. Justine just stared at him. For while he was laughing his face had been transformed from that of a cold-blooded devil to a wickedly attractive one. His black eyes gleamed and that hard mouth was softened by a display of dazzlingly white teeth.

'Very well, Miss Montgomery,' he said, a disturbingly charming smile still playing on his lips. 'I know when I'm beaten. Come to the bank first thing Monday morning and we'll work something out.'

Her mouth actually dropped open. 'You mean that? You honestly mean that?'

'I'm not in the habit of saying things I don't mean. You can have your loan, and your six months. Though not a minute more. Make no mistake about *that*! Now, perhaps we should get back to the party? Our hostess will be wondering what's become of us.'

'Oh, I can't stay now.' Justine was almost too excited to stand still. 'I have to go home and tell Mum. You've no idea how happy this is going to make her.'

Quite overcome with relief and joy, she rushed forward, reached up on tiptoe and kissed him on the cheek. 'Thank you, thank you, thank you, you darling man,' she gushed, and with one last dazzling smile, whirled and fairly danced out of the room.

Marcus stood there for a long moment, then reached up to touch the spot where her lips had rested. It was moist and soft, the only soft thing about him at that moment.

He had to laugh again, both at his fierce arousal and at the girl who'd caused it.

Darling man, indeed!

He knew exactly what she thought of him. He'd seen it earlier in her eyes. They'd been as contemptuous of him as he had been of her.

But money spoke a universal language with girls of her ilk. Come Monday morning she'd be smiling at him some more, smiling and flirting with him like mad, as she had yesterday in Hampton's office. No doubt he'd get the full force of her blinding charm now that she was going to get what she wanted.

After all, getting what she wanted was the name of the game for females like her.

But this time Marcus had every intention of getting what *he* wanted as well, which was the delectable and delightful Miss Montgomery.

There would be no question of bribing or blackmailing her into an affair. He would simply ask her out, as he would ask out any woman he was attracted to, then let things take their natural course.

Marcus had no doubt that Justine Montgomery would say yes to his dinner invitation, and whatever he wanted for afters. She would be keen to keep in good with her banker, especially once she saw how difficult it was going to be to make those monthly repayments. If there was one thing he could rely upon, it was that she would do *exactly* what he predicted.

Six months, she'd demanded. Well, six months

should just about do it for him, he decided cynically.

He recalled what Felix had said that first night he'd set eyes on her.

'You don't have to marry the girl...'

He finally appreciated the wisdom behind Felix's advice. He was so right. He didn't. If and when he ever contemplated marriage again it would not be to a girl who'd been brought up to think that a huge house was her birthright, along with a designer dress for every occasion.

Marcus wondered what she would wear on Monday. Not that lime-green dress again. Something more sophisticated, and subtle. She would want to impress him with her sincerity, and her seriousness.

Black, he guessed. Women always wore black when they wanted to be alluring without being obvious.

A knock on the study door was followed by Felix popping his head inside. He glanced around before coming into the room. 'Ivy said you were in here with Justine Montgomery.'

'I was.'

Felix's eyebrows rose and Marcus smiled a wry little smile. 'No, nothing like that, Felix. We were just discussing business. Miss Montgomery is in need of a loan.'

'Yes, so I'd heard. Trudy told me. She also said you'd already knocked Justine back but that you'd both been in here so long she thought Justine must have moved on to plan B.'

Marcus stiffened inside while he kept his eyes calm. 'Plan B?'

'A back-up plan if Justine didn't get that loan. Plan B was to find herself a rich man to marry in a hurry.'

For some reason, confirmation of Justine's character irked Marcus more than it should have. He'd already known what she was, hadn't he?

'I haven't forgotten how attractive you found her once before,' Felix was saying. 'I thought perhaps you might have been acting on that attraction...'

'Sorry to disappoint you, Felix. I was only offering Miss Montgomery that loan, not seducing her.'

'That's surprisingly generous of you, Marcus, considering her less than ideal circumstances. But you don't fool me, old chap,' he added, smiling lasciviously. 'You're usually hard-nosed when it comes to banking business, but I suspect it's passion, not compassion which has spurred you to such an uncharacteristic gesture. And she *did* look delicious in that red dress, didn't she?'

'I'm afraid I didn't notice what she was wearing, Felix,' Marcus said with a deadpan expression as he walked towards the study door.

Felix followed Marcus out of the room, laughing.

CHAPTER SIX

JUSTINE was kept waiting an unnervingly long time before she was ushered in to see Marcus Osborne on the following Monday morning. She must have sat in his secretary's office for over half an hour, long enough for her to start worrying that he might have changed his mind about giving her the loan.

Trudy would have laughed at her concern. On the phone yesterday she'd inferred Justine had it made because their esteemed banker secretly fancied her. Where she got that stupid idea from, Justine could only guess. That girl was obsessed with sex. Marcus Osborne didn't even *like* her.

Oddly enough, Justine found it hard to fathom her own feelings towards *him*. Trudy had been way off the mark when she'd accused her of being turned on by the man. Justine was sure she wasn't, even though she conceded he'd looked strikingly handsome in that black dinner suit last Saturday night. And kind of sexy, in that darkly brooding fashion Trudy had mentioned.

Justine had thought about him often over the weekend, with mixed emotions. She still resented his deception of the previous Friday but she had to admit she no longer hated him. How could she, when he'd magnanimously changed his mind and given her the loan? What she seemed to want more than anything, now, was to make him change his mind about *her*. She wanted him to look at her with

61

respect, wanted him to see she wasn't stupid or lazy, that she *did* have some character.

But she feared that was going to be hard to do. He had preconceived ideas about girls like her. She could see that. It worried her a lot that in the time which had elapsed since Saturday night Marcus Osborne might have reconsidered his impulse to give a loan to someone he obviously believed was superficial and possibly irresponsible.

Once Justine got the nod to go in to his office, that worry soared. She plastered a bright smile on her face and bravely ignored the butterflies in her stomach as she walked in.

The room was a far cry from the small walled cubicle he'd filled so intimidatingly on the previous Friday. Huge and rectangular, it was dominated by an equally huge semicircular desk behind which curved a complementary semicircle of glass.

In the middle of this circle, with his back to a view of the city skyline, sat Marcus Osborne.

He looked every inch the president of a prestigious merchant bank, his suit much more stylish than the pompous pin-striped number he'd sported for their last interview. Charcoal-grey and possibly Italian, it was a single-breasted two-piece with a sheen similar to its wearer's sleek black hair. His tie was an elegant grey and blue stripe, his shirt as white as his teeth.

His hard dark eyes surveyed her slowly as she crossed what felt like an acre of grey carpet. Justine might have been wrong but she gained the impression her appearance pleased him, and her confidence received a well-needed push in the right direction. She was glad now that she'd taken her mother's advice and dressed conservatively in a neat little black suit with short sleeves and brass buttons down the front. Her hair was up in a classy French roll and stylish gold earrings graced her ears.

'Sorry to keep you waiting, Miss Montgomery,' he said from his large leather chair. 'Do sit down.' He waved towards the group of three smaller upright chairs facing the desk.

She beamed at him as she selected the middle one. 'Please don't keep calling me Miss Montgomery,' she said sweetly as she crossed her legs. 'I hate that kind of formality. Call me Justine.'

His smile soothed her nerves some more. He wouldn't be smiling if he was going to knock her back a second time.

'Delighted,' he said. 'And you must call me Marcus.'

'Marcus,' she repeated, smiling her relief at the way things were going. She could not have borne to go home today and tell her mother it had all fallen through again. The poor darling had been so excited by the good news on Saturday night. It had totally revitalised her. She'd been a real help to Justine yesterday, mucking in with the housework, and even cooking dinner. Adelaide had also promised to do all the cooking for their boarding house venture, which perhaps was just as well, Justine thought ruefully. Cooking was not her forte. Though she could always learn. She'd told Marcus she could do anything when she put her mind to it, and so she could!

'You haven't changed your mind, I take it?' she asked.

'Not at all,' he returned smoothly. 'When I give my word, it's as good as my signature.'

'That's wonderful!' she exclaimed. 'I was a bit worried you might have. I suppose there are forms I have to sign?'

'Not at this juncture. And it's your mother who'll have to sign, since she's the legal owner of the house. I called you in to get some more details of your plans. First of all,' he went on, leaning back against the leather chair, 'exactly what contents are you going to sell to reduce the debt?'

Justine was glad she'd come fully prepared. 'I've made a list,' she said, diving into her handbag and extracting a folded piece of paper. She stood up to slide it over the wide desk. 'There are several items of antique furniture, some eighteenth-century silver and six paintings by well-known Australian artists. I've put a fair price against each item. As you can see, the total comes to over three hundred thousand, though naturally some of that money would be lost in commission at auction.'

She watched with some satisfaction when his face showed surprise. 'You have some very fine pieces of furniture here. And these paintings are exceptional.'

'You know something of antiques and paintings?'

'I've made an in-depth study of most investment methods. Really good antiques and paintings never lose their value, I've found, provided you don't pay too much for them in the first place. Who bought these? Your mother?'

'No, my grandmother.'

'Who did you get to price them for you?'

'No one. I priced them myself.'

When his eyebrows rose, she added, 'My grandmother was quite an expert and gave me an extensive education in art and antiques before she died.'

'I have to admit I'm impressed, Justine. *Very* impressed.'

Justine shone under his compliment. 'I'll contact an auctioneer this very afternoon,' she told him, anxious to impress him some more.

'No, don't do that. I'd be interested in buying what you have here myself. That way both of us get a bargain by avoiding commission.'

'But that's marvellous!'

'Naturally I would like to see them first. Would you be home this afternoon? Say around two?'

Justine hesitated. She'd been going to sell her car this afternoon. Still, that could wait. No way was she going to knock back an offer like this! Not only would it save her a lot of work, but Marcus was right; it would save her a lot of money.

Her smile was eager. 'Yes, of course.'

Yes, of course, Marcus thought wryly. He had no doubt she would say 'yes, of course' to pretty well any of his suggestions, including the dinner invitation he would smoothly slip in towards the end of the afternoon.

So far she'd been totally predictable, from the little black suit she was wearing to her whole demeanour. She hadn't wasted any time getting them on a first-name basis, and in throwing around some more of those dazzling smiles of hers. All the contemptuous glowers of last Saturday night had been banished, her eyes stopping short of outright seduction but showing a definite eagerness to please.

Admittedly, that list with its prices attached *had* come as a genuine surprise. The girl knew her subject. So did he. Marcus wasn't a fool. He recognised a bargain when he saw it.

Maybe this uncharacteristic episode in his life wouldn't cost him as much as he'd been fearing. For of course he could not actually give her that crazy loan with bank money. They'd think he'd gone mad! He would have to finance it through his own personal pocket.

But what the hell? he thought recklessly. She enchanted him, despite everything. Enchanted and aroused him unbearably. It was as much as he could do to sit here, acting the cool, controlled banker. He felt anything but controlled in her company. His mind would not give him any peace. It kept wandering to tonight, to that moment when he would at last have the opportunity to draw her into his arms and kiss her.

Unless, of course, an opportunity arrived earlier...

'Excuse me for a moment, Justine,' he said abruptly.

He pressed a buzzer on an intercom system, his secretary answering straight away. 'I'd like you to cancel all my appointments after lunch, Grace.'

'*All* of them?'

Marcus could understand Grace's shock. He'd never taken an afternoon off.

Well...not since that day he'd gone home on a hunch and found Stephany in bed with her lover.

The memory popped into his mind with all its

usual explicitness, but oddly enough there was no accompanying pain, and hardly any bitterness. His amazement was only exceeded by his gratitude towards the exciting young creature who was even now looking at him with a flatteringly focused interest.

A lot of people had told him that the way to forget Stephany was to find someone else. It seemed they'd been right. Not that he planned on marrying her. He wasn't *that* much of a fool. If darling Justine had actually moved on to plan B with him—and it *was* possible—then she was doomed to disappointment. Still, the fringe benefits of her trying to hook him were insidiously attractive.

'Yes, Grace,' he said firmly. 'All of them.'

'Very well, Mr Osborne. Oh, before you go...'

'What?'

'Gwen just rang. She's had a little accident. Sprained her ankle. The doctor says she'll be off her feet for a fortnight. She said to tell you she'd miss you. Anyway, I'll organise a temp to fill in, but I thought you'd want to know.'

'Yes. Thank you. Ring the florist, Grace, and send her some flowers. Include a note saying Marcus hopes she makes a swift recovery and that he's already looking forward to her return.'

'Yes, Mr Osborne.'

Marcus turned off the intercom and glanced up, startled to see Justine frowning at him. It came to him that she might be puzzled over his sending flowers to some woman who declared she would miss him. He didn't *have* to explain, but he didn't want her to have any reason whatsoever to reject him as a potential husband or lover. No way did he want her thinking he had some other lady-love in his life. The only lady-love Marcus wanted in his life for now was Justine herself.

'Poor woman,' he said. 'She's one of my cleaners. Does this room every night. Cleans this whole floor, actually. We often have a chat when I work late. Her husband is unemployed at the moment and she has five children. So she's the sole breadwinner.'

Marcus looked at Justine across his desk. To give her credit, she could adopt a sweetly sympathetic face when required. Truly, she could look almost angelic at times.

'Oh, dear,' she murmured. 'That's tough. Will she get sick pay?'

'Yes, of course. She's regular staff.'

'Let *me* do her job while she's away!'

Marcus was stunned by her request. And quite put out. Good God, the last thing he wanted was for her to spend every night cleaning his damned bank. He had other plans for her evenings.

'You don't know what you're asking,' he said curtly. 'Gwen cleans this whole floor. She works from six till midnight five nights a week. It's very hard work.'

'You think I'm afraid of hard work?' she flung at him, clearly affronted.

He didn't think she was *afraid* of it. She just had no idea what it entailed.

'Well, I'm not!' she insisted. 'I can do it. I know I can.' She leant forward in the chair in an appealing fashion, her lovely face both eager and enchantingly earnest. 'The university doesn't go back for another two weeks. I intend to put an ad in next Saturday's *Herald* offering full board. I would imagine I'll get plenty of takers, given the convenience of our house to the campus, but we won't be getting any money in for three weeks at least. I could do with two weeks' pay, I can tell you.

'Please, Marcus,' she pleaded, when he said nothing.

He stiffened as her use of his first name curled around his heart like a clinging vine, squeezing out feelings he'd never wanted to feel again for any woman. His immediate reaction to this unexpected weakness was immediate and fierce. He didn't want her touching his heart, damn it! The only part of him he wanted her touching was much lower.

Suddenly there was a perverse appeal in the image of her down on her hands and knees, cleaning and polishing the surfaces where he walked, and sat, and leant. It kept her firmly where he wanted her kept. In his carnal desires. Nothing deep or dangerous.

Marcus saw now that an intimate little dinner date tonight would have been a mistake. They'd have talked too much. He didn't want to get to know her—except biblically. There was no reason why he couldn't conveniently work late these two weeks, no reason why he couldn't have her in his office instead of his bed.

'Very well,' he said, fighting to keep his equilibrium in the face of his wildly flaring desires. 'You can have the job.' He flicked on the intercom before his conscience could get the better of him. 'Grace? Forget about finding a temporary cleaner. I have someone here willing and able to do the job. She'll be right out with her particulars. You can take her down to Personnel and sign her on as a casual.'

'Yes, Mr Osborne,' Grace said dutifully.

'You *are* willing and able, aren't you, Justine?' he couldn't help saying in slightly mocking tones. Though it was himself he was mocking.

You've lost it, Marcus. You've finally lost it.

She bristled at his tone. 'I told you once that I could do anything if I set my mind to it. You didn't believe me then and I see you don't believe me now.'

'Seeing is believing, Justine.'

Her blue eyes narrowed, and that lovely bottom lip of hers jutted forward. 'Yes,' she pouted. 'It will be, won't it?'

CHAPTER SEVEN

'YOU'RE going to work as a *cleaner*!'

Justine prayed for patience. 'Only for two weeks, Mum,' she said, and walked across the kitchen to open the refrigerator. She hadn't long been home from the bank, and desperately needed a cool drink. It was terribly hot outside.

She found a can of chilled cola in the door. The last one. She'd have to go food-shopping soon or they'd be eating the paint off the walls!

'But...but,' her mother was stammering in the background.

'But what?' Justine said frustratedly, only just managing not to slam the refrigerator door.

'Do you think you'll know what to do?' Adelaide asked uneasily.

'Oh, not you too!' She ripped the ring-top off the can, then tipped it up to her mouth.

'What do you mean? "Not you too..."'

The cold cola didn't cool her temper, which had been steadily rising along with the day's temperature. It had been the hottest summer on record for a hundred years, according to the silly weather man her mother devotedly listened to every evening.

'Marcus doesn't think I can do it, either. But I'll show him,' she vowed. 'I'll show him if it's the last thing I do!'

Justine threw some more cola down her throat.

'Marcus?'

71

'Marcus Osborne,' she elaborated irritably. 'The president of the bank. The man at Felix's party the other night. The man I saw today. Mr Sanctimonious! My God, what I wouldn't give to wipe that superior smirk off that disgustingly handsome face of his.'

'*Disgustingly* handsome?'

'Yes!'

'How old is this disgustingly handsome man?'

'Mid-thirties or thereabouts. It's hard to say. Sometimes he looks younger, sometimes older.'

'Married?'

'You're just as bad as Trudy!' She shook her head in exasperation then downed the rest of the cola.

'Really? In what way?' her mother asked vacantly.

'She's trying to marry me off to him as well. She thinks he fancies me, which is as far from the truth as you can get. I embarrassed him into giving me the loan the other night and now he probably regrets it, but he's too much of a gentleman to go back on his word. He thinks I'm an irresponsible nitwit and he's waiting for me to fall flat on my face. I dare say the only reason he's offered to buy the paintings is to prevent his looking a fool for giving me the loan in the first place!'

'He's going to buy the paintings?'

'*If* he likes them. He's shown interest in the antiques as well. He's coming here this afternoon to look at them.'

'What if he doesn't like them?'

'He will. Men like Marcus Osborne measure

everything in profit and loss. All those things are bargains, Mum, and well he knows it.'

'You really don't like him, do you?'

Justine thought of him, sitting in that big leather chair, looking oh, so impressive, but oh, so supercilious. 'He rubs me up the wrong way.'

'Is that all. Well, he's a man, dear, isn't he? Men often rub women up the wrong way. It's the nature of the beast. But it's often the most annoying men who are the most attractive. From what you've said about him, being Mr Osborne's wife would be a much better job than being his cleaner.'

Justine laughed. 'The day I become Mrs Marcus Osborne I'll walk naked down the aisle!'

Her mother gave her an irritatingly knowing little smile. 'That should make for an interesting ceremony, darling. You'd better wear a long veil.'

'Very funny, Mum.'

'I'm not trying to be funny. It's just that I've never seen you so rattled by a member of the opposite sex. Usually you're very *laissez-faire* about them while they're running around in circles trying to impress you. Are you sure your Mr Osborne isn't trying to impress you, but in a more subtle, grown-up kind of way? Since he's in his mid-thirties, then he *is* a man, darling, whereas all your other admirers have been mere boys.'

Justine gritted her teeth. 'Mum, I will only say this one more time. Marcus doesn't fancy me. He isn't trying to impress me. He's a banker through and through, with ice where his blood should be. The only woman he's ever really fancied, I'll bet, is Dame Nellie Melba!'

'He's into opera?'

'He might be, but that's not what I meant, Mum. Melba happens to be one of the lucky ladies who grace our bank notes! I'm sure he kisses her image goodnight every evening. Now, no more talk about our esteemed banker. All that does is raise my blood pressure, along with my temperature. I'm going to go have a long, cooling shower and find something negligible to put on before I dissolve into a puddle.'

Marcus pulled up outside the Montgomery residence in his pale grey Mercedes and looked over at the house. It wasn't a mansion, but it was a distinctive two-storeyed stone residence, sitting on a large block and surrounded by a lovely garden. It was also at the bottom of the street backing onto a bushland reserve which overlooked the Lane Cove River. It would bring well over a million at auction in this prestigious North Shore suburb, and in such an attractively private position. Justine was right. He was on a certain bet lending money with such a desirable property as security.

Feeling not at all soothed by this knowledge, he opened the car door and was immediately assailed by the heat. Everyone had been complaining about the long, hot summer, but weather didn't bother Marcus in the main. His life was mostly spent indoors and in air-conditioning. His house and his car were air-conditioned, as was the bank. He did go sailing on a Sunday, but you never seemed to feel the heat on the Harbour.

Despite the blistering afternoon sun, he dismissed the momentary temptation to take off his jacket and tie, determinedly ignoring his discomfort as he strode across the pavement and let himself in through the front gate. He sighed with some relief once he reached the shade of the portico, though the long wait for someone to answer the doorbell didn't do much for his composure. Beads of perspiration started forming on his forehead, which he dabbed at ineffectually with his pocket handkerchief.

His discomfort increased when the door was wrenched open and there stood the daughter of the house, wearing nothing but the shortest of denim shorts and a strawberry-coloured tube-top. Her lovely face was scrubbed free of make-up and her long blonde hair lay darkly damp and tangled across her bare shoulders, suggesting a recent shower and shampoo. A hairbrush in her hand, plus her dismayed expression, showed he'd taken her by surprise.

'You're *early*!' she accused.

'It's right on two by my watch.'

The grandfather clock which stood in a nearby corner suddenly started to strike the hour.

'Oh, my God, so it is. Sorry. Time seems to have gotten away with me. I *was* going to change before you arrived.'

Change? He didn't want her to change. He wanted her to stay exactly as she was, although it *was* a struggle to keep his eyes cool as they brushed over her bare shoulders, then dipped down to take in the disturbingly explicit outline of naked breasts beneath the ribbed red top. Difficult not to stare at her prominent nipples. Downright dangerous to think what he'd like to be doing to them.

'There's no need,' he said, a touch thickly. 'What you're wearing is fine.'

'It's certainly a lot cooler than what I was wearing this morning. Aren't *you* hot, dressed like that?'

Marcus's smile was strained, to say the least. 'I have felt cooler,' came his huge understatement.

'Then come inside and take your jacket off, for heaven's sake.'

Swallowing, he came into the relative cool of the cavernous foyer and allowed her to help him out of his jacket.

'*And* that silly tie,' she added, and held out her hand.

He imagined he wasn't the first man she'd encouraged to undress. Neither would he be the last, he kept reminding himself. 'Are you sure you won't tell on me?' he said wryly as he tugged the tie loose and lifted it over his head.

Her beautifully defined eyebrows arched in surprise, possibly at the flirtatious note in his remark. 'Is there anyone to tell? Aren't you the big boss at that bank of yours?'

'Yes and no. I *am* the president of the bank, but I don't own it. I'm answerable to the board.'

'I presume the board demands their president always wears a suit during work hours?'

'They would view my dressing casually with disapproval.'

She gave a dry little laugh. 'I'll just bet they would. But the board's not here, is it? You're playing hookey for the afternoon. From the sound of that secretary of yours this morning, you don't play hookey all that often, do you?'

'I'm a novice at the game, I must admit.'

'Well *I* was an expert when I was at school. The first hookey-playing rule is that you dispense with your uniform. No one can have fun wearing a uniform. Now give that tie to me. I have a feeling you'll put it back on as soon as my back is turned.'

He obediently placed it in her hand then watched as she hung both the jacket and tie in a coat closet under the stairs. Marcus's mouth dried at the sight of her from the rear. Truly, those denim shorts should be registered as a lethal weapon, along with that devastating top!

'And the second rule?' he asked on her return, congratulating himself on his outward composure.

'Oh, there isn't really a second *rule*. What comes next is up to the individual. You just go with the flow. Playing hookey is all about doing what you want to do instead of what you *should* be doing.'

'And what was it that you wanted to do when you played hookey, Justine?'

She smiled a rueful smile. 'Ah, now that would be telling. You already think I'm the silliest most irresponsible girl who ever drew breath. I don't want to give conviction to your suspicions. Let's just say anything was preferable to going to school on the days we had Mrs Bloggs for personal development and sex education classes.'

Marcus watched the way her mouth twitched with amusement, the way her eyes lit up with wicked pleasure at the memory. No doubt she hadn't needed any classes in either subject. She'd preferred to substitute practical experience for the theory.

He wished he'd been a boy going to *her* school around that time. He'd have gladly played hookey with the delectable Justine. There hadn't been any girls in the institution for boys he'd attended. No lady teachers, either. The place had been staffed by hard-nosed brutal teachers who hadn't heard that the laws regarding corporal punishment had been changed.

But he didn't want to think about that now. He wanted to focus his attention on this deliciously irrepressible creature whose path he'd fortuitously crossed.

He could no longer judge her harshly. She was what she'd been brought up to be. But there was no evil in her. No malice or cruelty. She wasn't another Stephany. She was like a breath of fresh air wafting in the window of his boring banking life.

All of a sudden he was sick and tired of the bank, sick and tired of working eighteen-hour days. He wanted to have fun, wanted to play hookey...with *her*.

He might have pulled her into his arms then and there, might have kissed those lovely lips senseless if a woman hadn't suddenly appeared in the hallway—a woman Marcus guessed was Justine's mother.

She looked him up and down as only a mother can. 'Mr Osborne from the bank, I presume?' she said, coming forward with her hand outstretched, and smiling suddenly. 'How do you do? I'm Adelaide Montgomery. Justine's mother.'

'How do you do, Mrs Montgomery?' He shook her plump little fingers while taking in her general appearance.

Overweight and overdressed, she was the perfect example of a pampered lifestyle. Still, for all her obvious over-indulgence, Adelaide Montgomery possessed a childlike charm in her smile which belied her background and made one instinctively like her.

'Oh, do call me Adelaide. Justine and I don't stand on ceremony, do we, darling?' she said, linking affectionate arms with her daughter.

'In that case, call me Marcus.'

'What a wonderfully masculine name! Well, I'll love you and leave you in Justine's capable hands, Marcus. She can take you around and show you everything. I just wanted to say hello and thank you for helping us out like you have. It's men like you who renew one's faith in humanity. *And* bankers,' she added with another of those sweet smiles.

'Don't forget to speak to Tom when he arrives, Mum,' Justine murmured, and her mother's face fell.

Marcus was wondering who Tom was when the older woman looked wistfully up at him.

'Tom's our gardener,' she said. 'At least, he *was* our gardener. Justine says we can't afford him now,' she added in a soft and heart-wrenchingly sad little-girl voice. 'I don't know how I'm going to bear to tell him he's not wanted any more...'

Marcus almost opened his mouth and offered to pay for the damned gardener himself, so great was this woman's ability to stir his long-dormant male protectiveness. Not like her daughter. She stirred *other* male feelings.

'Mum, I don't think we need discuss this in front of Marcus,' the girl herself muttered in a tight-lipped fashion.

Her mother reacted with a guilty fluster. 'No. No,

of course not. Sorry. You're so right, darling. Forgive me. I forgot. We have to solve our own problems.'

'Yes, Mum. We do. Now, I must get on with showing Marcus Grandma's things. I have to go to work tonight, remember?'

'Yes, yes, of course. I'll see you later, perhaps, Marcus? We might have afternoon tea together.'

'I'd like that,' he said.

Justine's mother went off down the hallway, looking chastened. Marcus felt angry with Justine, till he looked at her and saw her own distress. He suddenly appreciated the magnitude of her problems, plus the immense responsibility she'd taken on her slender shoulders.

His urge to pull her into his arms was no less strong, but now his desire was mixed with some sympathy. He wanted to soothe as well as seduce, which was not exactly an easy mix and did not sit well with him.

'Sorry,' she sighed, on seeing his frown.

'You've no reason to be sorry,' he said brusquely. 'I understand what you meant now. She's not strong, is she?'

'No.'

'She wouldn't be able to cope if she had to sell, would she?'

'Not very well. Come on, I'll take you upstairs and show you what's there first.'

She took off at a pace, Marcus hurrying to keep up. He didn't say anything till they reached the landing. 'About the garden, Justine...'

'No!' she said sharply, spinning round to face him. 'I don't want your charity, Marcus. You've already done more than enough. Mum might not be able to cope but I can. I'm young and I'm strong. I can mow a lawn if I have to. And weed a garden bed. Or don't you think I'm capable of that, either?'

'I think perhaps you're taking on far too much,' he prevaricated.

'Maybe I am and maybe I'm not. But that's for me to decide, isn't it? Or do you think I need some man to hold my hand?' she snapped at him.

He thought what she needed was a man's hand across her backside!

'I think what you need, Justine,' he said instead, 'is a friend.'

'A friend!' she snorted. 'I'm afraid friends have been a little thin on the ground around here since Daddy died. I used to have loads of friends. *And* boyfriends. But there's not one I could even ask to mow the lawn now. Not that I would!'

Marcus frowned. This was not what he'd been expecting. He'd thought any pass he made would have been readily accepted, and even encouraged, not misunderstood. Hadn't she flirted shamelessly with him since his arrival?

What game was she playing now? Hard to get?

He was forced to bypass the subtle for the straightforward. 'What about me?' he suggested.

'*You!*'

Her stunned surprise irritated the death out of him. 'Yes, of course. Who else did you think I was talking about?'

CHAPTER EIGHT

JUSTINE was floored. 'But... But...'

'But what?' he said smoothly. 'Is there any reason why we can't be friends, Justine? You just admitted there wasn't any jealous boyfriend in the wings who would object. As for my part, I am safely divorced, with no other lady-friend in my life at the moment.'

His dark gaze roved over her and Justine's stomach flipped right over. She wasn't a fool. He didn't mean a friend like Trudy was her friend. He meant boyfriend. Though 'boyfriend' seemed a highly inadequate word for a man like him. 'Lover' was more like it.

Marcus Osborne wanted to be her lover.

Good God!

Trudy had been right all along. Marcus *did* fancy her. He'd probably given her the loan and offered to buy the paintings and antiques *not* because he was fair, or compassionate, but because he lusted after her.

Which made him not much better than Wade Hampton, really. He was simply more devious.

Justine should have been outraged. The girl who'd gone to the bank last Friday would have been. The girl who'd swanned into Felix's party on Saturday night would have torn strips off him. The girl who'd visited him this very morning at his office would have reacted with disgust.

82

But something had happened to that girl since then. Lord knows when, or how. Her mother had been right when she'd said Marcus rattled her more than any member of the opposite sex ever had. He did.

She'd certainly acted out of character from the moment she'd opened the door just now. She'd babbled on, flirting with him in a way, and actually undressing him to a degree. Had she done that because subconsciously she'd wanted to touch him, wanted to see if the breadth of his shoulders was real or just clever tailoring?

They had felt real enough.

She stared at him now and wondered what he'd look like without any clothes on at all. The thought flustered her even more. She could feel the blood in her veins heating, flushing her throat and her face.

Dear heaven, had Trudy been right about this as well? Could it be that underneath her fury and irritation she'd been sexually attracted to Marcus all along?

Disbelief warred with reality, which was that the thought of Marcus lusting after her, wanting her so badly that he would do anything to have her—lower his standards, break his precious rules, risk his self-righteous soul, even—quite blew her away.

Her bewilderment was total.

'Justine?' he prompted. 'Is there a problem?'

'Why would you want to be my friend?' she blurted out. 'You don't even like me.'

Their eyes met and she could not tear her own away. His suddenly smouldering gaze held her effortlessly, mercilessly, sending her pulse-rate wild.

'Justine,' he said thickly, and reached out to run the fingertips of his right hand down her cheek.

She could not move, her eyes widening as his head bent, closing the distance between his mouth and hers. He was going to kiss her, and she was going to let him.

Justine squeezed her eyes tightly shut, as though by closing them she could almost pretend this was not happening to her. She couldn't possibly be going to stand there and let Marcus do this. It was unthinkable!

A small moan escaped her mouth as his lips brushed hers. When he lifted his mouth away, another moan followed, a strangely pained protest. The thought that he might leave it at such an appallingly brief kiss brought a rush of dismay so intense that she reached up on her toes and pressed her lips back against his.

He groaned. Immediately his hand, which had been hovering lightly against her face, slid down around her throat to firmly cup the nape of her neck, holding her mouth captive under his. His other hand snaked around her waist, settling in the small of her back and pulling her hard against his body. She was pinned to him, their bodies touching everywhere, chest to chest, stomach to stomach, thigh to thigh.

It felt incredible. *He* felt incredible. His body, his heat, his mouth moving restlessly over hers. She'd never experienced anything like it, had never known a kiss could evoke such a wave of excitement and longing. She wanted more, more of the kiss, more of him. Her mouth flowered open with a tortured little moan this time. And he needed no further invitation.

His tongue darted forward, then dipped deep.

Where other male tongues had previously brought revulsion, his brought a raging, reckless rapture. She could not get enough of its driving hunger. When he went to withdraw, her hands clutched at his shoulders and she claimed his lips back with hers, sending her own tongue into his mouth with a desperation which would later stun her.

Marcus finally wrenched his mouth away and wrapped her to him, hard. 'Remind me not to kiss you anywhere in public,' he rasped into her hair, his chest heaving against hers. 'Hell, Justine...'

Justine didn't agree. This wasn't hell. It was heaven.

'Kiss me again, Marcus,' she whispered, and lifted her face up to his.

He cupped her face and started kissing it all over. She closed her eyes once more and sucked in breath after breath of much needed air, little 'ohs' escaping her mouth when he pressed his lips to each eyelid.

'God, I want you,' he said thickly, and returned to her parched, panting mouth at long last. 'Tell me you want me too,' he insisted, while his lips hovered over hers and she was simply dying with anticipation and excitement. 'This isn't just gratitude, is it? Tell me this is real, Justine. Tell me!'

'Yes,' was all she could manage, her head spinning, her heart pounding. 'Yes,' she repeated, and melted into his mouth once more.

Elation crashed through Marcus when he heard her admission and felt her surrender. No one, he thought triumphantly, could pretend that well. She wanted him, wanted him as much as he wanted her.

His kiss was hungry and demanding, her response everything he could have wanted it to be.

Dear God, but she was a highly sexed creature. The sounds she made. The way she moulded her body to his. He could only imagine what she would be like when he was inside her. Just thinking about it sent his own arousal into overdrive.

His arms tightened to lift her slightly off her feet and sweep her from the landing into a nearby room, his mouth never leaving hers. It was a bedroom, he noted out of the corner of his eye, a large bedroom with a huge four-poster bed. He pulled her down with him onto the cream-quilted bed, and tried not to think of her mother downstairs.

Soon, kissing her mouth wasn't nearly enough. He had to touch and taste the rest of her. His passion was out of control. *He* was out of control.

So, it seemed, was she.

She didn't stop him when he peeled that provocative little top down to her waist and exposed those perfect breasts to his eyes, and then his lips. She moaned and arched beneath him with an almost liquid abandon as he licked the soft pink nipples into pointed peaks of obvious pleasure. She gasped when he sucked one deep into his mouth and gave it a lover's nip, groaning when he released it.

'You like that?' he rasped, propping himself up on one elbow and staring down at her.

'Yes,' she admitted, her eyes wide upon him.

Yes, indeed, he thought ruefully as he made a concerted effort to get himself under control. As much as he would have adored to strip her totally, right here and now, common decency demanded he stop. Her mother could come upstairs at any moment.

But it was almost impossible to turn his back on the passing pleasure she offered. I'll stop soon, he promised himself, then watched her face while he trailed the back of his right hand across her exquisitely swollen breasts, revelling in her sharply inward gasps, exultant at the flaring of her nostrils whenever he contacted her still wet nipples. He took one between his thumb and forefinger, rolling it to an even more erect and sensitised state.

Her lips fell raggedly apart, her big blue eyes gradually growing heavy with desire. She looked lost on a sea of sensuality, utterly incapable of stopping either him or herself. He had no doubt she would do anything he asked, regardless.

Did she always respond with such total abandon? he wondered, the thought rattling him for a moment before he swept it ruthlessly aside. What did it matter if she did? This was what he wanted from her, wasn't it? Sex on tap till his mad desire for her had burnt itself out. Who cared what she did with other men? The last thing he wanted was to become emotionally involved with the girl.

'Justine!' her mother suddenly called up the stairs. 'Are you up there?'

Marcus swore under his breath, deserting her to swing his feet onto the floor and stand upright. Justine, he noted wryly, took several seconds to snap out of it. When she did, she sat bolt-upright, blushing furiously as she yanked her top back up over her still betrayingly aroused breasts.

Marcus almost smiled at that blush. It seemed

even the most liberated girl found embarrassment in the face of possible discovery by a parent. Did that sweet mother of hers think Justine was still an innocent little virgin?

Marcus imagined Grayson Montgomery hadn't been under any such illusion about his daughter when he'd been alive. Such a man of the world would have recognised her inherent and undoubtedly well-explored sensuality. *Any* man would.

Marcus watched her frantic straightening of the quilt, noting ruefully that she was unwilling to meet his eyes. He actually found her guilty fluster quite enchanting, perhaps because it was so at odds with the wanton creature who a moment before had been lying there, naked to the waist, oblivious to everything but his hands upon her.

'Justine?' her mother called again, her voice decidedly closer.

CHAPTER NINE

JUSTINE groaned, gave the quilt one last agonised glance and dashed for the landing, determinedly avoiding Marcus's darkly amused eyes.

'Right here, Mum. What do you want?'

Her mother was halfway up the stairs, puffing. Justine felt more than a little breathless herself. She thanked God her mother had called out instead of coming up first.

'Tom's here. We'll be out in the back garden if you want us. How are things going with Marcus? Did he like what you had to show him?'

'I certainly did,' Marcus answered, coming up to stand next to her on the landing, his hands reaching out to curve over the railing.

Justine went hot all over as she stared at those hands which a minute before had been doing such incredible things to her. She could still feel her nipples burning beneath her top.

'Excellent,' Adelaide chirped, and waddled back off downstairs.

Justine stood frozen by Marcus's side, confusion rampant within her. Common sense warned her this wasn't true love come at long last. Not in a million years!

Her feelings for Marcus were extremely powerful all the same. And very disconcerting. What she'd felt on that bed had been mind-blowing. She'd never experienced anything as exciting, despite not feeling comfortable with being so out of control.

Marcus didn't seem to be suffering from any such confusion. Or discomfort. Once her mother had disappeared, he turned her straight away and took her into his arms once more, kissing her till her head was reeling.

'Are you always like this with women?' she asked breathlessly when he finally let her mouth go.

'Like what?'

'So…wicked.'

He laughed. 'Now, that's the pot calling the kettle black, isn't it? I didn't notice you stopping me in there. Or now.' He trailed kisses across her cheek to her ear, blowing softly within.

'You do things to me,' she admitted, shuddering wildly. 'Things I've never felt before…'

'In what way?'

'In *every* way.'

'Mmm. Tell me more,' he murmured, and bent to nuzzle her neck.

'Maybe it's you who should be telling *me* more,' she said huskily.

He straightened and stared down at her with narrowed eyes. 'What are you talking about?'

'Did you give me that loan because you wanted to get me into bed?'

'Will I get my face slapped if I say yes?'

'No.'

'Then, yes. I did. In part.'

Again, disgust was very much absent from her reaction, even with his admitting the worst. She thrilled to the evidence of his passion for her, a passion which must have gone against his grain.

She hadn't forgotten that he didn't think too highly of her.

'I fought the temptation from the moment I saw you last Friday,' he confessed wryly as he ran a tantalising fingertip around her mouth. 'I might have succeeded if you hadn't been at that damned party, wearing that damned dress. Do you know how you look in that red dress? Do you have any idea what it did to me?'

'No...' How could she? Today was the first day she'd been introduced to the pleasures of the flesh. But she'd glimpsed its power now, and could well understand the compulsion to put aside thoughts of right and wrong in exchange for such pleasures.

'Come with me now,' he urged darkly, his finger trailing down her throat towards her still aching breasts, 'and I'll show you.'

'Now?' she repeated breathlessly.

'Yes. We can go to my place. It's not all that far. No one will be there. We'll be alone.'

As much as she wanted to, the image of herself surrendering her whole body to Marcus, of his taking her virginity, of his finding out she *was* a virgin, brought a wave of sheer panic.

'I...I can't do that.' She whirled out of his arms and away from his disturbing touch.

'Why not?' he demanded sharply. 'You said you wanted to earlier. What's changed all of a sudden?' His face hardened, his black eyes glittering coldly. 'Don't start playing the tease with me, Justine. I'm not in the mood and it doesn't suit you.'

'I'm not. I just...you're...you're rushing me. I *hate* that!'

One of his eyebrows arched, and a sardonic smile

twisted his mouth. 'You want to make me wait, is that it?'

'I...I think I want to make *myself* wait.'

'Ah...'

She had no idea what that 'ah' meant, except that it sent a startlingly sexual shiver running down her spine.

'And you call *me* wicked,' he murmured. 'All right, have it your way. When will you go out with me, then?'

When...

Justine knew his asking her to go out with him was the same as his asking her to go to bed with him. It was a fair enough presumption, she supposed. She'd led him on, no doubt about that. And, in truth, she wanted Marcus to be her first lover. She could see now that her waiting for true love was a silly romantic dream, fuelled by a belief that she would need an incredibly deep and special love to surrender her body in total intimacy to a man. She'd thought in terms of making a sacrifice, never participating in the act for pure pleasure.

What she'd felt with Marcus this afternoon already was pure pleasure. Well...maybe not so pure...but definitely pleasure—pleasure she could not turn her back on.

But along with a natural fear of the big event lay a fear she might scare him off, once he discovered her lack of experience. Justine could see he thought her a right raver. It was an understandable conclusion, given the way they'd met and the circles she moved in. Virginity was a rarity. Promiscuity more the norm. These days boyfriends *expected* to sleep with their girlfriends—maybe not on their first date, but sooner or later.

Marcus was a mature man. He wanted a mature sexual relationship with her. He would move on to another more willing woman if she said no.

Justine was amazed at how sick that thought made her feel.

'When, Justine?' he growled.

'Saturday night,' she blurted out.

'Saturday night! My God, that's an eternity away. Why not tonight?'

'I have to work tonight, remember? And every night this fortnight.'

'Damn! I knew that was a bad idea when I agreed. Look, what say I arrange for someone else to do it? We can spend each evening together, instead. I'll give you any money you need.'

'No.'

'What do you mean, no?' he demanded irritably.

'I mean, no, you are not going to arrange for someone else to do my job. And, no, you are not going to give me any money at all! I aim to earn what money I need in life. Legitimately. As I told you once before, I don't go to bed with men for money.'

Oh, no? Marcus thought cynically. He doubted he'd be here with her at all if he wasn't who he was, with a bank at his disposal.

'You also said wild horses wouldn't get you into bed with me,' he pointed out dryly, watching for a sign of guilt, looking for any evidence that her passion was not mutual but merely practical. After all, if she wanted him as much as she seemed to, why the delay in consummating their desire for each other?

In truth, he doubted her asking him to wait was an erotic game, designed to increase the intensity of her sexual satisfaction. He'd found the games women played were more about power than pleasure. *He* was the one to be teased unbearably by the wait, to be brought to a pitch where he would do anything she asked just for release. He wondered if she'd already moved on to plan B, wondered how much was real and how much was just an act.

No matter, he thought darkly. Saturday night would come. And, by God, so would he!

'I think I should get on with showing you the things you came to see,' she said abruptly, before throwing him a troubled glance. 'That's if you really *do* want to buy them. You're not going to confess you only came here this afternoon to seduce me, are you?'

Seduce *her*? What a laugh that was! She needed about as much seducing as Mata Hari. He'd never known a woman to go up in flames so quickly. In hindsight, he could not possibly see how she could have faked that scenario on the bed. Her body spoke an automatic and instinctive language under his touch. He had been its master there for a while. My God, the way her nipples had sprung upright at the lightest touch. The way she'd moaned. And writhed.

Hell, he had to stop thinking about that, or he'd end up in the funny farm by nightfall, let alone by Saturday night!

'I'm not going to confess another single thing,'

he growled. 'I take it you won't reconsider my suggestion to give this a miss for now?'

'You take it correctly!' she pronounced firmly.

'Then let's get on with it,' he muttered.

It was a very trying afternoon. Marcus found it hard to keep his mind on proceedings to begin with, though once he recognised the value of what he was being offered his long-trained mercenary nature came to the fore.

The paintings she showed him were by well-known Australian artists, and quite rare. Worth every cent she'd put on them, and possibly more. The antiques were just as rare, mostly small and quite unique tables. There was an eighteenth-century walnut and rosewood inlaid gaming table that would have brought a small fortune at auction. The workmanship was so outstanding Marcus felt guilty taking it for the price. When he said so, however, she waved a dismissive hand.

'I'm happy with the price I put on everything. I'm also happy thinking that they're going to someone who will value them. I know you'll look after Grandma's things as I would have, especially the paintings.'

'They're yours, Justine?' he asked, frowning. 'Not your mother's?'

'Everything I've shown you is mine. Grandma left them to me in her will. I didn't like to sell Mum's things. She's lost enough already.'

He was touched, and at the same time perturbed, especially when it looked as if she was suddenly fighting back tears. 'Justine, if you don't want to sell these things, please say so.'

'There's no question of wanting to, Marcus, but

having to, I'm afraid. It's either this or lose the house, and I know Mum couldn't bear that.'

He frowned further. Was she manipulating him here? Angling for more of his help? Playing on his sympathy? She claimed she wanted to survive on her own, but was that true?

Plan B popped into his mind again. A wealthy husband would solve all her problems. Marcus was almost tempted to offer himself, since she wouldn't take his money otherwise. Wives didn't seem to have any trouble spending their husbands' money.

But the possibility she might say yes, plus the inevitability of another divorce, kept his mouth firmly shut on that subject. As Felix had once told him oh, so wisely. 'You don't have to marry the girl...' He didn't. He just had to wait till Saturday night. Meanwhile, he would offer an option for her to repurchase any of her grandmother's things in the foreseeable future, since he would be keeping them as an investment for some years to come.

'Justine, I...'

'Please don't go making any new offer I'm going to have to refuse, Marcus,' she snapped. 'I only took your loan because I believe I can pay it back. And I accepted your offer to buy these items because I knew you were getting your money's worth. No charity was involved, simply a fair exchange. You once told me there was no quick and easy way in life. I believe you now. Daddy's death has made me face lots of things about myself. Yes, I was a spoiled little miss with a silver spoon in my mouth. I never had to do without, or budget, or work for a living. But I'm learning. And I'll learn more, if you let me.'

She drew herself up tall and set uncompromising eyes upon him. 'You want to be my friend? Fine. I'd like that. You want to be my boyfriend? That's fine too. I'll bet you're great in bed. What I don't want is for you to become my sugar-daddy. That I *don't* need. Okay?'

He was impressed, both by her speech and her sentiments. As long as they were for real...

'Believe me,' he said, 'the last thing *I* want is to become is your sugar-daddy. I wasn't going to offer you money. I simply wanted to say thank you.'

She gave him a wary look. 'For what?'

'For giving me the opportunity to possess and enjoy some very unique treasures. I promise to look after them for you, and if you ever want to buy any of them back again, they're yours at the same price.'

Her eyes flooded with tears and she looked away, blinking rapidly.

Marcus could not help but be moved. She was a more deeply feeling girl than he'd previously given her credit for. He actually began to believe that everything she was doing wasn't so much a matter of selfishly clinging to a comfortable lifestyle, but out of genuine caring for her mother and her home.

He placed a comforting hand on her disturbingly bare shoulder, but didn't say anything. Words were impossible as he battled the urge to haul her into his arms once more.

She threw him a brave smile through soggy lashes. 'Sorry,' she said, and dashed away the last of the tears with the back of her hand. 'It's not like me to be weepy. Thank you so much for that offer.

That's one I won't refuse. You're so right. Grandma's treasures *are* unique.'

Marcus let his hand drop away from her satiny smooth flesh, his stomach contracting at the thought that the most unique treasure of all he wanted to possess and enjoy was Justine Montgomery herself. He just hoped the price was not going to be too high.

CHAPTER TEN

'No!' TRUDY gasped over the telephone after Justine had related a slightly edited version of the day's events. 'I don't believe it!'

'But you were the one who said Marcus fancied me in the first place!' Justine protested.

'That's not the part I don't believe, silly. It's your fancying him *back* I don't believe.'

'I know. I find that hard to believe myself. He's just left and I simply *had* to tell someone. I couldn't tell Mum. She's still got Tom with her.'

'Who's Tom?'

'Our gardener.'

'I thought you said you couldn't afford a gardener.'

'We can't. But he's insisting on doing it for nothing. He says he doesn't need the money and that he would be at a loss without the work. I have a feeling he's sweet on Mum. He's a widower, you know. I think she likes him too. She was all atwitter over afternoon tea. And she didn't gush over Marcus like I thought she would. Tom got all her attention.

'Anyway, enough about Mum and Tom. I rang you up to talk about Marcus and me. I need your advice about something. Trudy, I'm going out with him next Saturday night and he's going to have a fit when he finds out I'm a virgin. I just know he will.'

'My God, you're going to sleep with him on your first date? I mean, this is *you* we're talking about, isn't it, Jussie, not me?'

'Yes.' Justine sighed. 'It's me.' She knew it sounded totally out of character, but she also knew she wouldn't be able to resist Marcus if he started making love to her.

And he would. She just knew he would! He hadn't wanted to take her to his house this afternoon to play chess!

'My God, what did he *do* to you today? Put a spell on you or something?'

Perhaps, Justine conceded. She was totally bewitched and besotted with the man. He'd filled her every thought since he'd left the house only fifteen minutes earlier. Yet already it felt like a lifetime.

'He's not what I thought he was,' she said. 'He's...he's...'

'A banker,' came Trudy's dry remark. 'Never forget that. And he was once married to the biggest trollop since Jezebel. Or so Father said. I didn't know her myself. Father says he's once bitten ninety times shy. He won't marry you, Jussie.'

'But I don't *want* him to marry me.' The very thought had never crossed her mind!

'This is *me* you're talking to, remember? I know you, Jussie. If you fancy the guy that much, I'll bet my bottom dollar you're already falling in love with him. Once you've lost your virginity to him you'll be head over heels and thinking about foreverland. Especially if he proves to be a good lover—which thankfully, I doubt.'

'He *will* be a good lover,' Justine said, quivering

at the memory of what he'd done to her on her
mother's bed.

'You sound very sure of that. Good Lord, what
did he do to you today? I don't believe this. I was
only joking the other night when I said you might
be turned on by that cold-blooded devil.'

'Marcus is not at all cold-blooded.'

'She's defending him now,' Trudy muttered on
the other end of the line. 'The other day she hated
him!'

'I was wrong about him.'

'Maybe you weren't.'

'I thought you'd be pleased. You've been at me
for ages to give sex a fair go.'

Trudy was disturbingly silent at the other end.

'I'm not in love with him!' Justine insisted.

'Mmm.'

'I see there's no point in asking for your advice,
then,' she snapped, and hung up.

The telephone rang back straight away and she
reluctantly answered it, knowing her mother was
out in the garden with Tom.

'I'm sorry,' Trudy said. 'I'm a bitch. But I don't
want you to get hurt. Look, I know I used to tease
you about your waiting for true love to come along,
but underneath I thought it was rather sweet.'

Justine's chin began to quiver. Before she knew
it, she'd burst into tears.

'Don't cry, Jussie,' Trudy begged. 'Please don't
cry.'

Justine got a hold of herself pretty quickly. Truly
she was having an emotional day. First she'd cried
with Marcus over her grandma's things. Now she
was crying over her lost romantic dream.

'I'm all right,' she sniffled. 'Really.'

'No, you're not. You've had a rotten time lately, and you deserve to have some fun. Go out with Marcus by all means, and go to bed with him, if you want to. Just keep a lock on that tender heart of yours. You're not made for casual sex, Jussie. If you were, you'd have been doing it all along.'

'He probably won't want me when he finds out I'm a virgin,' she wailed.

'I wouldn't be too sure of that,' came Trudy's dry reply. 'He might want you all the more.'

'Oh? I would have thought he'd run a mile.'

'Why?'

'Because my virginity will shatter all his preconceptions about me. Plus all his expectations. He disapproved of what I did at the bank last Friday, but he was tempted all the same. He believes I know my way around a man's bedroom, not to mention a man's body. He says he wants to be my friend, Trudy, but I think he only wants a fling with a young woman of the world!'

'Mmm. I think you could be right.'

'I can improvise with the foreplay part. I've read enough to have some clues. But that's not going to help much when it comes down to the act itself. I don't want him to know that I haven't done it before. Is there any way I can get around that?'

'Gee, Jussie, I don't know…'

'What happened in your case?'

'It hurt like hell.'

'Oh, golly.'

'But I have a girlfriend who swears her first time was a breeze. No pain. Nothing. There again, she was a mad horsewoman—switched to riding men with no trouble at all!'

Justine closed her eyes. This was a crazy and embarrassing conversation.

'This is silly, Trudy,' she said. 'Maybe I should just tell him the truth.'

'Perhaps that would be for the best.'

'You think he'll dump me then, don't you?'

'I think he'll think twice.'

'Good. That's what I want him to do. Last Friday at the bank I convinced him I was something I wasn't. I'd like the opportunity to redress that opinion.'

'You want his good opinion?'

'Yes.'

'Oh, dear...'

'I'm *not* in love with him!'

'I heard you the first time.'

'Nobody ever believes me,' Justine wailed.

'I believe you. Now, hang up, Jussie, or you'll be late for work. It's gone four-thirty. Didn't you say you had to be at the bank by six?'

'Yes, but it's not far. Only down at Chatswood.'

'Don't forget, it's peak hour traffic. He's not going to be there tonight, is he?'

'Marcus, you mean?'

'Who else?'

'I don't think so. He had the rest of the day off. Why?'

'Men like him always work late. Even later if they fancy the cleaner.'

'You have a wicked mind.'

'Yeah. And I'm only a girl. Imagine what kind

of mind a man of thirty-five has. What are you going to wear?'

'They supply an overall at the bank.'

'An overall's good. Very hard to undress a girl in an overall.'

'I'm not going to listen to any more of this.'

'All right, but don't say I didn't warn you.'

'I won't!'

'I'll ring you tomorrow. Better still, I'll drop round.'

'You do that. You can be useful for once and help me sell my car.'

'Sell your car! But you *need* your car.'

'I need *a* car, not one worth what mine is worth. I'm going to trade down and bank the difference. You've no idea how much it costs to live, Trudy.'

'Tell me about it tomorrow.'

'Don't come before noon. I'll be wrecked after tonight.'

'Mmm,' Trudy said salaciously.

'Oh, stop that!' Justine snapped, and hung up again.

Marcus had no intention of going back to the bank when he left Justine's place. He drove home and went for a long swim, which cooled his blood as well as his ardour. He climbed out after twenty laps, suitably deflated, dragged on a bathrobe and set about making himself a snack and some coffee. He switched on the television and settled back to watch the five o'clock news while he ate.

The newsreader came on. She was pretty and blonde, with a nice smile. But not a patch on Justine, whose face would launch a thousand ships...her figure, a million. He would never forget the sight of her perfect pink-tipped breasts, or the way those breasts had responded to him. He could still see her in his mind's eye, lying semi-naked on that luxurious quilt, her eyes shut, her lips parted and panting.

Marcus swore violently. He'd been doing quite well, trying not to think about her. Now she was back, tormenting his mind and his body. The thought that later this evening would find her alone in his office at the bank brought devilishly wicked temptations. He felt compelled to go there, to see her in the flesh. No one would think anything of his turning up, not even Justine. He had every reasonable excuse to return to the bank today.

'Had to work late,' he imagined himself saying to her when she came in. 'Missed far too many hours this afternoon.'

His smile was self-mocking. He wondered what she'd say if he told her what he was really thinking. 'Missed you already, sweetness. Can't wait till Saturday night. Care for a session on the boardroom table?'

No.

That was what she would say to him. No.

Marcus was not about to put himself into a position where he might look desperate. Or like a fool. Which meant he would just have to wait patiently till Saturday night before making his next move.

Clenching his teeth hard in his jaw, he pointed the remote at the TV screen and consigned the blonde newsreader to oblivion, then rose to get himself another cup of coffee.

*   *   *

Justine wanted to cry. She'd been stuck in a traffic jam for fifteen minutes, yet she was less than fifty metres from the tall blue glass building which housed the bank. A couple of times she'd been tempted to leave her car where it was and just walk. But she couldn't, could she? She was trading the darned thing in tomorrow. She *needed* the car. It was worth more money to her than two weeks' work as a cleaner.

Her insistence on doing this cleaning job that morning had been more a matter of pride and stubbornness than desperate need, despite what she'd said to her mother and Trudy. She'd wanted to show Marcus that she wasn't lazy, that she was prepared to work hard. And now she was going to be late.

Damn, damn and double damn!

At long last the car ahead moved, and although it was at a crawling pace the line of traffic eventually crept through the lights, where the presence of shattered glass all over the road indicated an earlier accident.

What rotten luck, Justine thought. Finally she was able to turn off the highway into the car park driveway. She whipped down the ramp, where she was stopped by a barrier and a security guard, who told her officiously that this was a private car park and not a racetrack. Justine kept her cool, flashed him one of her winning smiles, then showed him the pass the personnel manager had given her that morning.

'I'm a relief cleaner,' she explained. 'This is my first night. There was an accident up the road and it's made me late.'

The guard frowned at her expensive car, shrugged, then directed her to a reserved though now empty parking space in a corner by the lifts. She was only twelve minutes late on arrival on the sixth floor, where she hunted frantically for the cleaner who was supposed to tell her what to do and how to do it.

Justine located her in the very cubicle which had been the scene of her first embarrassing encounter with Marcus. After explanations and apologies, the woman—who was around fifty and called Pat—kitted Justine out in a grey overall and supplied her with a mobile cart full of cleaning equipment, along with a huge set of keys.

The seventh floor was her domain, she was instructed, and each room was to be securely locked after being cleaned. She was to start at the far end of the corridor, where the boardroom and the big boss's suite were, then work backwards. Vacuuming and dusting the rooms was on the agenda every night. *Nothing* was to be touched in any of the offices, except the rubbish bins which required emptying. Lastly, the washrooms were to be cleaned. There were four on the seventh floor. Mr Osborne had a small *en suite* bathroom attached to his office as well.

'I stop for a cuppa and a bikkie around eight-thirty,' Pat told her at the lift doors. 'I'll give you a call. Oh, and don't worry if some of the rooms aren't empty. The fellas in this 'ere establishment are workaholics and slave away into the wee small hours of the night. Just clean around 'em. They'll hardly notice.'

Pat gave Justine a sharp look. 'Er...I take that

back. A fella would have to be dead not to notice you, lovie. You'd better tie that hair of yours back. And don't smile too often. You only have five hours to get around the whole floor, and being chatted up is not on your list of jobs.'

Justine wound her hair up into an untidy and hopefully unattractive knot on the short ride up to the seventh floor, then wiped her lipstick off with the back of her hand. She hadn't come here to be hit upon by some yuppie bank executive. She'd come to clean, and to prove something to herself and Marcus.

The lift doors opened and she stepped out into the hushed corridor, pushing the cleaning cart before her. Pat had been right. There were lights on in a few of the offices. A door on her right suddenly opened and a man in a grey suit hurried past, not so much as giving her a glance. He looked very harried.

Was this what Marcus demanded of his employees? she wondered. Ten-hour days and tunnel vision? Was this what Marcus himself was like most of the time? She recalled how startled his secretary had been when he'd said he was taking the afternoon off. Obviously he didn't play hookey from work too often.

Her mind turned momentarily to his marriage and the reasons for its failure. Trudy had called his ex-wife a trollop. But Trudy called every second female a trollop! Maybe Marcus had never been home, and his wife had strayed out of neglect. Such things happened.

She would ask Trudy tomorrow to find out whatever she could from her father about Marcus's marriage and the woman he'd married. She wanted to know how long the marriage had lasted and how long it was since his divorce was finalised.

Justine recoiled at the sudden appalling thought that there might have been children involved. She didn't want Marcus to have children. Actually, she didn't want him to have had a wife, either. She certainly didn't like the idea of his ever having been in love before.

But he's not in love *now*, you fool, came the savage voice of reason. Certainly not with *you*! He's struggling to like you. He wants to get you into bed, darling. That's the bottom line. He admitted it. You tempted him last Friday and he finally acted on that temptation. Keep that thought in mind and don't start turning this into a romance. It's a matter of chemistry, not true caring, of lust, not true love.

Justine's stomach contracted, and her heart did as well. Oh, God... Was Trudy right? Was she falling in love with Marcus? Had she *already* fallen in love with him?

She didn't know. How could she? She'd never fallen in love before, had no idea what it felt like. Wasn't it more likely she'd fallen into lust? After all, whenever her thoughts turned to Marcus, sex was not far behind. She could not stop thinking about what it would be like, being with him. Saturday night could not come quickly enough.

Her resolve to tell Marcus she was a virgin wavered considerably in the face of the possibility he *might* run a mile once he knew her lack of experience. That was not what she wanted. Not at all. She wanted his mouth back on hers, and his hands, and every other part of his body!

A disturbingly erotic shudder rippled through her.

Dear God, this will never do, she decided shakily. She had to stop thinking about him or nothing would ever get done here tonight.

But not thinking about Marcus was impossible, especially once she pushed the cart down the corridor to the reception area where she'd sat that very morning, waiting to see him. Although the lights were still on, his secretary's desk was now unattended, her computer turned off, her chair pushed back.

Grace was not a young woman, a fact which had pleased Justine at the time. If his secretary had been a glamorous young piece Justine knew she would have been jealous.

Was jealousy a sign of love? Or just lust? Whatever, it was certainly a sign of feeling something. Boys had often accused her of being heartless over the years, of caring for no one but herself. Justine had shrugged off their accusations as sour grapes because she hadn't cared a whit about *them*. She would not have been jealous of any girl ensnaring Howard Barthgate, or any of the boys she'd gone out with. But the thought of Marcus admiring or being with any other female brought jabs of real pain.

Justine shook her head at herself. Lust or love, it was not a very nice thing to suffer from. She decided she didn't like it one bit!

Marcus lasted till twenty past six. His third cup of coffee was left to go cold on a side table while he dashed to his room and pulled on underpants before dressing in what came quickest to hand—a pair of grey trousers which had just been returned from the drycleaners and were hanging on the wardrobe door. He grabbed a navy silk shirt from his shirt drawer and fumbled appallingly with the buttons. Grey socks and black leather shoes proved not so difficult, but were still irritatingly time-consuming.

Another precious minute was wasted trying to put some order into his pool-damp hair, which had a tendency to kink and wave when wet. Usually he blow-dried it straight. Tonight he didn't have time, or the patience. Despite his rush, it was still twenty five to seven by the time he backed out of the garage and pointed in the direction of the Pacific Highway. As he accelerated away, he thanked his lucky stars that he'd bought a house close to the bank. Ten minutes and he'd be there!

Not quite. There must have been an accident earlier, for the traffic was backed up and moving very slowly.

Seven had come and gone by the time a very frustrated Marcus pulled into the underground car park under the concrete and glass skyscraper which housed his bank, only to have the security guard flash him an anxious look.

'Gee, Mr Osborne, you said you'd gone for the day. I...er...I let someone else use your parking spot. A new cleaner. Pretty little thing. She was running late because of the traffic. Sorry, Mr Osborne, but I didn't think you'd mind. The spot next to your usual is empty.'

He didn't mind at all—till he saw what kind of a car Justine was driving.

Marcus slid his Merc into the spot next to the sporty Nissan and glared across at the sleekly silver lines. He knew exactly what such a car was worth, especially one so new. Hardly the sort of transport a girl needed when she was down to her last dollar, when that very morning she'd begged to be allowed to work as a cleaner because she needed the money. Even if she didn't own the car outright, the insurance alone would be quite high, much higher than an ordinary little runabout which would have sufficed for her needs.

Clearly Justine wasn't about to compromise the parts of her life which showed her status to the world at large. Her home. Her car. Her wardrobe.

There was no longer any doubt in Marcus's mind that Justine intended to put plan B into action in the not too distant future. Everything else she was doing were merely stop-gap measures, designed to keep the wolf from the door till she could land herself that sugar-daddy husband she'd seemingly scorned.

But was the object of her manipulations yours truly? he speculated caustically. She was certainly working hard to change his bad opinion of her.

Marcus suspected, however, he was another stop-gap measure—someone to satisfy her highly sexed nature till a suitable marital candidate came along. She'd have to be a fool to think *he'd* marry her, given the manner of their initial meeting.

Justine Montgomery might be a lot of things, but not a fool.

No. She'd decided to kill two birds with one

stone, supplying herself with a lover while conveniently keeping him sweet over the loan at the same time. Then, when plan B succeeded, she would have done with both in one fell swoop.

Or maybe not? Marcus pondered darkly. Maybe, if he pleased her in bed, she might plan to keep him on as her lover. It would not be the first time an ambitious young woman had married one man to better her financial position while entertaining other males on the side.

Marcus rode the elevator up to the seventh floor with fire in his eyes, and in his belly. If Justine thought she could use him, then she had another think coming. It was *her* who was going to be used. Ruthlessly. Smoothly. Mercilessly.

CHAPTER ELEVEN

JUSTINE was finding cleaning more complex than she'd thought it could possibly be. There was so much equipment on her cart. Pat had assumed she knew what was used for what, and she did recognise some of the products, but the others required a good reading of the label before she understood their purpose and the right method of application, which slowed things down somewhat.

Marcus's washroom had proved more difficult than his office, but she was proud of the job she'd done and was standing in the doorway, admiring the sparkling surfaces and smudge-free mirror, when Marcus's face suddenly appeared in that mirror, right behind her left shoulder. She almost dropped the can of spray-on polish she was holding.

'My God, Marcus!' she exclaimed, whirling to smile shakily up at him. 'You almost scared me to death then. What on earth are you doing here?' she demanded to know while her eyes ran over his startlingly casual yet still elegant clothes. He looked sinfully sexy in that navy silk shirt, the open neck revealing a hint of dark hair on his chest. Justine had never thought she would like a hairy-chested man. Now it seemed a most desirable asset.

'I had to get something from my office,' he said, his dark eyes running over her in return, their expression dryly amused by *her* appearance.

In truth, the overall she was wearing was much

too big for her slender frame, and lacking shape altogether. A grey colour, it was like a boiler suit, with studs which snapped shut down the front from the neck to the groin.

'Yes, I know,' she said, a mixture of embarrassment and arousal heating her face. 'I look ridiculous. Pat couldn't find any smaller ones.'

'You still look a damned sight cuter than Gwen did,' he said, his eyes raking over her once more.

But not with amusement this time. A raw, naked passion blazed in their black depths, both shocking and exciting her.

She took a somewhat shaky step backwards, which he seemed to read as a silent invitation, for he followed her into the *en suite* bathroom and shut the door behind them. Justine just stood there like a frightened rabbit while he took the spray can from her frozen right hand and deposited it on top of the toilet.

She wanted him to kiss her, but she was afraid all of a sudden. There was a dark intensity about Marcus—an almost angry quality—which she found both unnerving and disturbing. But, for all that, she was powerless to stop him, her body already filled with a deep longing to feel his mouth and hands on her once more.

He obliged. Oh, how he obliged, kissing her with a hunger which rattled her brain and took her breath away while his busy hands were snapping the overall open and peeling it back till it fell off her shoulders and pooled onto the white-tiled floor, leaving her standing there in nothing but her joggers and undies.

It momentarily crossed Justine's befuddled mind

that her very sexy-looking pink satin half-cup bra and French knickers did not present a virginal image, neither did the way she suddenly began undressing Marcus with as much indecent haste as he'd stripped her.

His shirt buttons were proving decidedly difficult, so he simply ripped the shirt apart from under her fumbling fingers, sending buttons flying everywhere. Four frantic hands disposed of his trousers, Justine's eyes blinking wide at the size of the bulge in his underpants.

It was a sobering moment when he took her hand and held it to him, letting her feel the harsh outline of his stunningly large erection. There was no way, she realised, that he wasn't going to hurt her, no way she could hide her virginity. Not that she really wanted to. She wanted him to know how special this was for her, how special she found him. Whether it was true love or not didn't matter. It was still the first time any man had made her feel like this.

'Marcus,' she rasped, her tongue feeling thick in her mouth. 'I...I...'

'Don't talk,' he ordered brusquely, and bent to dispose of his underpants before straightening.

Justine could only stare in awe at the power of his naked male body with all its aggressive sexuality. Her mouth dried as she tried to imagine such a formidable shaft buried deep inside her, her heart stopping for a moment.

But then he took her hand again and wrapped it around his straining flesh, urging her to stroke its satiny length, to feel its strength as well as its strangely stirring vulnerability. She did what he wanted, and watched as his eyes closed on a moan of raw, ragged pleasure.

The sound found echoes in her own body. Soon she was burning with desire, any idea of saying anything that might stop him swept away by her own unstoppable yearnings.

When he pushed her downwards and pressed himself against her lips, she took him blindly into the heat of her mouth, no thought entering her head but that she wanted to please him, to give him pleasure. He stopped her all too swiftly, lifting her back up to cup her face and stare into her passion-glazed eyes with a hot and almost disbelieving gaze.

'You're a witch,' he growled, before his head bent to take a fierce possession of her lips, his tongue ravaging the depths of her mouth with a wild and frenzied passion. She gasped for breath when he finally abandoned her mouth, but there was to be no peace for the rest of her body. He grabbed her upper arms in a bruising grip and hoisted her up to sit on the vanity, pushing her legs apart and moving between them. He kissed her neck while he dragged her bra straps off her shoulders, peeling them downwards till the satin cups gave up their swollen inhabitants to his questing and quite ravenous mouth.

'Oh, God,' Justine moaned when he swept his tongue over each rock-hard nipple. Her back arched to offer her breasts up to be licked and sucked more easily; her hands pressed palms-down on the granite surface at her sides. Her eyes closed in ecstasy, her head tipping back, her lips falling softly apart. It felt better than it had that afternoon, the sensations electric and compelling. She panted his name, moaned her dismay when he stopped, her head snapping forward to dazedly watch him yank off her joggers then peel her panties down her legs.

Now she was totally naked, and he was parting her legs again, exposing her totally to his gaze. An intoxicating mixture of shame and excitement flooded Justine as he touched her there while watching her face. A wild heat claimed her cheeks, and her lips fell raggedly apart. But it was *him* she was soon wanting inside her, not those tormenting, teasing fingers which quickly drove her insane.

'Marcus...*please*,' she groaned, and actually moved her legs wider, begging him with her body as well as her eyes.

'All right, witch,' he said thickly. 'If that's what you want. But that won't be the end to it. Not by a long shot.'

She gasped her shock when his head began to bend towards the liquid fire between her legs. For that was not what she wanted at all! Naturally she'd read of such an activity, had heard Trudy wax lyrical about it. In truth, she was sure at some other time she might enjoy it with Marcus. But not right now, not when she was desperate to have him inside her, to hold him to her and feel their flesh as one. She was sure now it wouldn't hurt. His fingers had slipped inside her so easily. She knew she was very ready.

'No,' she groaned, and his head jerked upright, dark eyes startled.

'No?'

'No,' she repeated. 'Not that. Not right now. I want *you*, Marcus. Only you.'

'But I don—'

'Marcus, please,' she broke in, and cupped his face with her hands, using the leverage to slide her bottom to the edge of the vanity, wrapping her ankles around his hips and drawing him towards her. 'Do it. Now. I can't wait another moment.'

'God help me,' he groaned, and did what she wanted. Swiftly. Passionately. Roughly.

Justine couldn't help it. She screamed.

CHAPTER TWELVE

MARCUS sat at his desk, his head in his hands.

The sound of water running had his head slowly lifting. He stared at the washroom, with its firmly shut door, and thought of her pale, pain-filled face; of his own shocked self stumbling back from the vanity, of his staring down at the bright red spot on the white tiled floor.

He hadn't known what to do, or to say. Yet he *had* said something, hadn't he? Some thoughtless obscenity. And she'd looked up at him with such scorn in her eyes.

'Just go,' she'd flung at him, pressing her knees together and wrapping goose-bumped arms over her bare breasts. 'Get out!'

So he had. And now he was slumped at his desk, his largely buttonless shirt hanging limply around him, his mind in chaos.

But, good God, how could he have known, or guessed? Virgins didn't waltz into a bank and practically prostitute themselves to loans officers! Virgins didn't let men they hardly knew caress their bare breasts while their mothers were downstairs! Virgins didn't willingly go down on a man in a washroom, damn it!

Marcus groaned at the memory. Her sweetly eager lips had driven him instantly insane, had sent him hurtling towards that point of no return so that he'd had to stop her. Even then he'd been beyond rational thought, had succumbed to a recklessness totally alien to his character. When she'd begged him to just do it, he'd brushed aside his usual passion for protection to embrace a different passion, namely Justine Montgomery, the breathlessly beautiful, wickedly wanton, deliciously decadent daughter of the equally decadent Grayson Montgomery.

But the Justine Montgomery he'd thought she was didn't exist.

A virgin! He still could not believe it. How had it come about? How could a girl looking like her, responding as she did to a man's touch, reach almost twenty-two without having intimately known a male body?

Different if she'd been locked in a convent somewhere. Or been raised in a strictly religious community. The circles she moved in, however, were not exactly renowned for their shrinking violets!

The washroom door opened and Justine walked out with her head held high, her eyes still full of scorn.

'I was right about you,' she said, with more than a touch of bitterness. 'Trudy was wrong.'

Trudy? Now, why would Justine be talking to Trudy Turrell about her relationship with him?

Marcus's brain finally snapped back into gear.

Trudy Turrell.

Plan B...

'I said you'd run a mile once you found out,' Justine went on scathingly.

Marcus thought that would be a damned good idea, if good old plan B was at the bottom of all this. Had Justine been trying to trap him with a pregnancy just now? Had all her so-called eagerness been just part of the plan to ensnare a rich husband for herself? Had her seemingly stunning responses all been an act?

If they had, then by God, she was the greatest faker he'd ever met!

Yeah, right, Marcus, the cynical voice of experience argued back. You're God's gift to women, aren't you, my boy? They can't resist you. They always love you just for yourself, and never for what you can do for them. She couldn't possibly be faking it, could she? She's been saving herself just for you. Waiting for Mr Right to come along before she gives herself in true love.

Huh! And I'm Little Lord Fauntleroy!

The more likely truth is that she's a mercenary ex-rich bitch who's always seen her virginity as a marketable commodity to be bargained with, or sold to the highest bidder in marriage. Don't forget her silver car, that cynical voice reminded him. And her home. And her designer clothes.

She wants it all. *That's* the bottom line. Let's face it, Marcus, her fancying you *was* very sudden, and so very, very convenient, wasn't it?

Marcus's heart hardened with his thoughts.

No female was going to make a fool of him a second time. Yet, dear God, he still wanted her—maybe more than ever. No matter what her motives, the thought of being her first lover, of taking that beautiful body and bending it to his will, was incredibly arousing.

But there would be no pregnancy. And no marriage.

'You should have told me,' he said.

She looked away from his searching eyes, hugging herself defensively. 'So it seems.'

'Why *didn't* you, Justine?' he persisted, wanting to see if she could come up with a smooth lie, instead of the truth about plan B.

She shrugged. 'What does it matter now?'

Marcus had his answer. He was amazed at how much it hurt.

Her eyes were mocking as they turned to meet his. 'I presume Saturday night is off?'

After all she'd put him through? Hell, no! He stood up and walked smoothly over to her, congratulating himself on his own acting ability. His arms curled over her shoulders and he looked down into her immediately wary eyes. 'Now, why would Saturday night be off?' he murmured, the warm smile on his face belying the coldness in his heart.

'You're...you're *not* going to run a mile?' she asked, with what might have been a heart-wrenchingly touching manner...if it had been genuine.

'Of course not. Now that I'm over my initial shock, I find myself enchanted by the thought of your not ever having been with another man. My only regret is that I was so rough with you just now. Though you have to admit my assuming you were a woman of the world was hardly my fault, my love,' he added, with just the right amount of gentle reproach.

She blushed delightfully. Now, that was a skill worth having, he thought cynically. Being able to conjure up a blush at the drop of a hat.

Aware of his still simmering frustration, he bent to press light kisses to her cheek, her nose, her mouth, struggling all the while not to be taken in by the soft gasps of seeming delight she made.

'I...I should have told you,' she confessed breathlessly against his lips.

'Mmm. Never mind. No harm done.' Now he kissed her properly, though still carefully restraining his hunger. Damn, but she was a good kisser, he conceded, marvelling at the way she let her body melt into his, at the way she seemed so desperate for his tongue in her mouth.

And who knew? Maybe, having held her sexuality in check for so long, she was now unable to control it. Perhaps Pandora's Box had been well and truly opened. It was a tantalising thought, and one which Marcus would savour for the rest of the week.

'You're not angry with me?' she managed to say between kisses.

'Not in the slightest,' came his quite truthful reply. For anger was no longer his prime emotion at that moment. Hell, he had to get out of there fast or he'd be right back where he started, and still without any protection at hand.

But it was Justine who stopped the kissing, drawing back to stare up at him with gratifyingly glazed eyes. 'I...I must get back to work, Marcus.'

'Must you?' Already his body was demanding he coerce her back to his place, where he could be alone with her at his leisure.

'Please don't try to stop me,' she said shakily, as though reading his mind.

'*Could* I?' he drawled.

'You know you could. But if you like me at all, Marcus, please don't. Not now. Not tonight.'

Her voice broke, as if she was on the verge of tears. As he looked down into her glistening eyes Marcus felt his own heart squeeze tight.

Hell, he agonised, and looked away quickly. Not that. For pity's sake, not that.

He whirled to stalk back behind his desk, buttoning the one remaining button on his shirt and tucking the tails firmly into the waistband of his trousers. 'Very well,' he said curtly. 'I have to do some work myself, anyway. Though I think I should do mine at home, don't you? Remove myself from this occasion of sin.'

'Occasion of sin?' she repeated blankly.

'That's being within touching distance of you, darling Justine,' he said drily. 'If you'd spent time in St Andrew's Home for Wayward Boys, you'd know all about occasions of sin, and the many ways us wayward boys encountered them. You had "occasion of sin" written all over you from the moment you walked into this bank. My blood pressure still hasn't recovered from that lime-green dress you were almost wearing.'

Damn, she was blushing again. How did she do that? The guilt it evoked in him was incredible! What he needed was a change of subject. And a change of scene.

'Before I go,' he said as he swept up his car keys from the desktop. 'What day can your mother come into the bank to sign all the papers for the loan?'

'Oh. Um. Any morning this week, I suppose. I could drive her in.'

In the silver sports, he thought acidly.

'I'll have Grace ring you tomorrow to confirm,'

he said. 'She can also arrange a mutually convenient time for the removalist to come.'

'Removalist?'

His irritation knew no bounds. What was wrong
with the girl? Where had her brains gone to all of
sudden?

'For the paintings and antiques, remember?' he
said. 'I'll get Grace to make the arrangements and
give you the details when she rings.'

'Will *you* ring me tomorrow?' she asked.

One of his eyebrows automatically lifted. 'Do
you want me to?' he said, wondering what she was
up to now. Maybe she'd changed her mind and
wanted to see him sooner than Saturday night. If
she did, then that might mean she really wanted
him. Him, Marcus. Not him the high-profile president of a bank and potential partner for a gravy-
train life.

'Yes, of course.'

There was no 'of course' about it. She was beginning to confuse him again.

'Right,' he said testily.

'Why do you say it like that?'

'Like what?'

'Like you're angry.'

He sighed. The last thing he wanted was to make
her suspicious of *his* motives. 'Justine, love,' he
said. 'I'm not feeling too good right now. Men
don't like to be taken that far and then have to stop.
Sorry if I was short with you, but I'm in considerable discomfort. It's called frustration, not anger.'

'Oh.'

That damned blush again! And it worked every

time, making him question everything he believed about her.

'I think I'd better go,' he said.

'Oh, Marcus, I'm so sorry,' she apologised, and took a tentative step towards him.

His fists clenched into balls at his sides lest he surrendered to the temptation to take her in his arms once more.

'I'll ring you tomorrow,' he promised, then marched determinedly from the room.

'I told you he'd show up at the bank last night,' Trudy said scathingly on the way to the used-car lot. 'I'll bet he didn't go there to work at all. I'll bet it was just to seduce you. Which he seems to have done with surprisingly little resistance from you, I might add. I'm surprised you're making him wait till Saturday night to finish what he started, if you were enjoying yourself that much!'

'I am too,' Justine had to admit. 'But you've no idea how much it hurt, Trudy. One minute I was in ecstasy, and then in agony. I thought it would take me at least the rest of the week to recover.'

In more ways than one. She'd been in shock afterwards, both physically and emotionally. It had taken her some considerable time to get her thoughts and feelings together. How she'd finished her cleaning job after Marcus left, she'd no idea. When she'd finally arrived home she'd run herself a bath and lain in its soothing warmth for ages before going to bed.

Unfortunately, although exhausted, she hadn't been able to sleep, the memory of Marcus's love-making fuelling her mind and re-inflaming her body. She'd tossed and turned for hours in a ferment of frustration and longing. Lust, like fire, she finally accepted, could be a good servant but a very bad master. She could well understand why Marcus had been so irritable afterwards.

'Well, if you'd told him you'd never done it before, like you said you were going to,' Trudy hissed, 'then it wouldn't have hurt so darned much. He'd have known to be more gentle. From the sound of things you'd been acting like you'd been doing it since puberty, so what did you expect? On a vanity! Good Lord! You've truly shocked me, Jussie.'

'I shocked myself, believe me.'

'You've certainly got it bad. Either that, or Marcus is a far better lover than I had him pegged.'

'I told you he'd be a good lover.'

'Yes, well, maybe I was wrong there. But I wasn't wrong to warn you off him. Dad says he's very bitter about his first wife. He says you've got very little chance of marrying Marcus Osborne!'

'Trudy! How many times do I have to tell you? I have no wish to marry Marcus. I don't love the man; I just want him to...to...'

Justine tried not to colour guiltily when her friend flashed her a truly scandalised look.

But she wasn't about to be a hypocrite. Or a naïve fool. By morning, she'd accepted that her feelings for Marcus were strictly sexual. What she was suffering from couldn't possibly be love. Love was warm and tender and sweet. Love was safe and secure. It didn't hurtle one along darkly compelling tunnels into a world where shame and excitement mingled to ignite one's flesh into uncontrollable flames, where you begged mindlessly for the burning to be stoked even further, where only the most excruciating pain could douse that seemingly unquenchable fire.

Justine had no doubt that Marcus could take her back to that point of no return whenever he wanted, and the next time there would be no excruciating pain to stop proceedings. The barrier of her virginity was gone, banished to the wilderness where once she'd walked in total ignorance of the pleasures of the flesh. She'd tasted the full potential of those pleasures now, and there would be no going back.

Still, having discovered the intensity and power of her sexuality, Justine found the future a little frightening, and somewhat confusing. Her feelings about Marcus were often mixed up. Saturday night seemed both too close and too far away.

'Do you think we might abandon the subject of men and sex for the next hour?' she said impatiently as she eased her Nissan over to the kerb outside the first of the used-car lots she planned to visit. 'I have a car to trade in.'

Trudy was about to argue when she spied a salesman walking in their direction. A very tall, very handsome salesman. Her switch to seduction mode was focused and immediate.

Justine shook her head as her friend bolted out of the car. Trudy had a hide accusing *her* of acting in a promiscuous fashion! Marcus was her first lover whereas this poor, unsuspecting salesman would probably become another victim in Trudy's hapless male harem!

* * *

Three o'clock that afternoon found Justine the proud owner of a neat white seven-year-old Pulsar, plus a sizeable change-over cheque, which she banked before coming home and finding the rates notice in the mail. She rolled her eyes at the amount, and slid it in the drawer where she kept all the other unpaid bills. At least now she had enough in her account to cover all their living expenses for a few months, with some rainy-day money left over.

'Mum!' she called out. 'Where are you?'

'Out here, darling,' came the lilting answer from the direction of the back yard.

The sight of her mother on her hands and knees in the garden, happily weeding, surprised Justine. Not so much the sight of Tom, standing nearby watering, and watching her mother with the tenderest look on his face, his eyes soft, his smile sweet.

Justine's heart turned over, then twisted slightly. Now, *that* was the look of love, not the darkly glittering gaze Marcus had bestowed upon her last night. Or that smoulderingly sexual smile which sent her into a tailspin.

'Hello, Justine,' Tom said on seeing her.

'Hi, there, Tom. It's hot again today, isn't it?'

'Not as bad as yesterday. But we could do with some rain. The gardens are beginning to suffer, what with the water restrictions and all. You can only use a hand-held hose during the day, you know. No sprinklers.'

'It's been a long, hot summer all right.'

'Yet we're only at the end of January.'

'Still, you've got the garden looking lovely, Tom. I'm only sorry we can't pay you.'

'You couldn't pay me for what I get while I'm

here, my dear,' he said softly, so that her mother could not hear.

Justine didn't say a word, just smiled at him. He smiled back, and Justine thought what a really nice man he was. He had lovely eyes. A soft brown, they showed intelligence and kindness. He was not as handsome as her father, but still a fine figure of a man.

Her mother glanced up from her weeding, her face rosy-cheeked, her pretty blue eyes sparkling. 'Did you and Trudy find a nice new little car, dear?'

'Not new, Mum. But little, and much more economical. And Trudy found herself a nice new boyfriend.'

'That girl! Speaking of boyfriends, Marcus rang earlier, by the way,' she added with a knowing little smile. 'He said he'd ring back.'

'That's nice.' No use denying Marcus was about to join the boyfriend category. She just hoped her mother didn't start thinking an engagement ring and wedding bells were to follow.

Despite her attempt at cool sophistication, the sudden sound of the telephone ringing sent Justine's heart leaping and her stomach contracting.

'That'll be him now, I don't wonder,' her mother said. 'Aren't you going to go in and answer it?'

'Yes, but it's too hot to hurry.' Justine took her time, not picking up the receiver in the hallway till the phone had rung a dozen times.

'Hello?' she said nonchalantly.

'Miss Montgomery?' a woman's voice answered.

Justine's instant and very intense disappointment showed what a fool she was to think she could play at being a woman of the world. The truth was she'd been dying to hear from Marcus all day, to feel reassured that he still wanted her after sleeping on his discovery that she was a virgin.

'Yes,' she said rather wearily. 'Who is this?'

'Grace Peters here. Mr Osborne's secretary. I've organised a removalist to call at your house Friday morning at ten, Miss Montgomery. Does that suit?'

'Yes. Yes, that's fine.'

'And Mr Osborne can see Mrs Montgomery to-morrow morning at eleven, if that suits as well?'

'Yes, that should be fine too.'

'Splendid. Now Mr Osborne would like to speak to you himself. I'll just put you through.'

'Justine?'

She clutched at the phone. Just his voice was doing worrisome things to her body, especially her knees.

'I'm ringing, as asked,' he said on a drily teasing note.

'Yes. So you are.' She was astonished at her coolly composed reply. Amazing when she was in danger of dissolving onto the carpet. Still, if she was going to have a strictly sexual affair, then it was imperative she keep a semblance of control over the situation.

'I did ring earlier but you weren't home,' he volunteered. 'Your mother said you were out shopping with Trudy. Since I can't imagine that particular young lady being acquainted with supermarkets I assume you were conducting an end-of-summer raid on the Double Bay boutiques?'

Justine pulled a face at the sardonic note in that last remark. Obviously Marcus still thought she was an irresponsible idiot, using what little money she had left on clothes. 'I don't have the money for such frivolities as fashion,' she pointed out. 'If you must know, I was busy trading in my car for a cheaper model.'

Silence at the other end.

'Marcus? Are you there?'

'Yes. Yes, I'm here. Sorry. Grace came in for a second. What was that you were saying? Something about trading in your car?'

'Yes. I've been going to do it for ages. Dad bought me a silver Nissan for my twenty-first last year, you see. Paid cash for it, which was darned lucky, otherwise it would have been repossessed like poor Mum's car. But it was an unnecessary expense to run and maintain. The insurance alone was horrendous.'

'So what did you buy instead?'

'A used Pulsar.'

'Did you have it inspected?'

'No. Why should I?'

'Did you get a warranty with it?'

'Twelve months. Oh, for pity's sake, don't go all macho male on me and start asking me a million mechanical questions about the darned thing. It's a car with four wheels and will get me from point A to point B and that's all that matters. You're the one who said I should live within my means and that's what I'm doing.'

'Mmm.'

'What does ''mmm'' mean?'

'It means I wish I could see you tonight.'

Justine's breath caught in her throat. 'I...I wish you could too.'

'God, Justine, I—'

'No, Marcus,' she broke in. 'I have to go to work. Stop trying to tempt me.'

'What about tomorrow? Meet me for lunch.'

A quickie at lunchtime? Oh, no. That was not what she wanted at all! 'No, Marcus,' she said firmly. 'Saturday, and not before. Pick me up at seven.'

'Seven...'

'Is that too early?'

'No,' he said drily. 'Not nearly early enough— unless you're talking about seven a.m.'

'I'm not.'

'I didn't think so. In that case I won't be ringing you again before then. It's far too...disturbing.'

The thought of him sitting behind his desk in a state of acute arousal gave Justine a perverse jab of pleasure. She didn't stop to analyse too deeply why she wanted him to suffer, but she did. Maybe she wanted some revenge for his propelling her out of her innocent and largely happy world, where sexual passion and frustration had been alien concepts and emotions.

'In that case, don't *you* work late any night this week,' she said tartly. 'Because I find *that* disturbing!'

'Mmm. Now, that's a very provocative confession, Justine. Brings all sorts of possibilities to mind about desks and deliciously polished boardroom tables.'

She flushed at the images he evoked. Thankfully, he couldn't see her flaming cheeks.

'I think your board of directors would expect their esteemed president to restrict his activities in that room to mergers of a more financial kind, don't you?' she countered.

Marcus laughed. 'We'll see, Justine. We'll see. I'll give you a reprieve for this week. But I won't promise the same for next week. That might be a different story.'

Justine couldn't even begin to think about next week. Saturday night was as far as her thoughts would extend at that moment.

'Will you be coming in with your mother in the morning?' he asked.

'Do you need me?'

'Would you care to rephrase that?'

'Is my presence strictly necessary?'

'No.'

'What a pity! I was about to iron my lime-green dress.'

'I'm not sure if I'm relieved or disappointed. That dress exposes more leg than your shorts did yesterday.'

'Not to worry. I'll wear it on Saturday night, if you like. I might have to, anyway.'

'What do you mean...have to?'

'Well, if this heat keeps up, I have the stunning choice of the lime-green or the red silk I wore to Felix's party. They're the only summery dresses I kept.'

'Kept?'

Justine bit her bottom lip. Darn! She didn't want Marcus to think she was crying poor-mouth, or looking for pity.

'Justine? Explain, please.'

When Marcus got that tone about him, there was nothing to do but obey. 'Look, I had to sell most of our going-out clothes to get some cash for food, and to pay the phone bill, otherwise I wouldn't be talking to you now. It's not a big deal. Mum and I didn't need dozens of glam dresses, anyway. I didn't expect to be going out much for a while, to be honest, so if we're to date on a regular basis then you'll have to put up with seeing me in the same things over and over, I'm afraid. Sorry.'

'There's no need to apologise, Justine,' he said tautly. 'No need at all.'

'Good, because I didn't mean to. It's a habit with females, that's all, saying sorry all the time when there's absolutely no need. Though I *was* sorry I hadn't told you I was a virgin last night.'

His sigh could have meant anything, but Justine automatically concluded it meant something bad.

'If you want to call it quits,' she said sharply, 'then just say so.'

'I don't want to call it quits.'

'Then what's the problem?'

'Who says there's a problem?'

'You sighed.'

His laugh was dry. 'So I did.'

'Well?'

'A sigh is just a sigh, Justine. Don't read so much into it. I'm tired. I didn't get much sleep last night. I doubt I'll get much sleep for the rest of the week.'

'Oh.' She quivered at the thought of his lying wide awake in bed, thinking of her, wanting her, needing her.

'Marcus,' she said, and her voice was low and husky.

'Yes.'

'Don't be late on Saturday night.'

'Don't worry,' he said ruefully, 'I won't be.'

CHAPTER THIRTEEN

HE *WAS* late. Seven minutes. But it was enough for
Justine to have a taste of how she would feel if he
never came, or if he ever decided to wipe her from
his life altogether.

Devastation did not begin to describe her feelings. She spent those interminable seven minutes
pacing to and fro across the lounge room and peer-
ing anxiously through the curtains, grateful that her
mother was relaxing in a bath upstairs after her
afternoon's gardening, unable to witness her daughter's uncharacteristic agitation.

Justine tried telling herself that sexual frustration
was the reason for her fear-filled state, but some-
how that didn't wash. Realisation dawned once
Marcus pulled up in his Mercedes and she almost
burst into tears with relief.

'Oh, my God, I *am* in love with him!' she wailed
aloud.

Dropping the curtains, she clutched her bag to
her chest and tried not to cry. Though whether it
was from delight or dismay now, she wasn't sure.

Get a grip on yourself, girl, common sense demanded very quickly. So you're in love with him.
That's nice. But he's not in love with you, so don't
go winding romantic dreams around him. Trudy
warned you good and proper. He's not going to
marry you. All he wants is an affair. Right? Got
that? Good!

137

An artificially composed Justine went to answer the doorbell at seven minutes past seven, having schooled her face into a perfectly understandable pout. She swung open the front door, ready to lambaste him for being late, but her words of reproach died at the sight of him.

He was wearing black. All over. Not the bleak, funereal black of that pin-striped suit he'd been sporting at their first meeting. A devilishly dark and sleek black, which screamed sin and sex from every angle.

She tried to keep the hunger out of her gaze as it swept over him, absorbing each wickedly elegant detail.

Lightweight woollen trousers proclaimed Italian tailoring. A black silk shirt, with long sleeves and an open neck. Shoes and belt fashioned in black leather. Combined with his flashing ebony eyes and sleek black hair. He looked like every woman's fantasy of a bad-boy lover come true.

It took several seconds for Justine to appreciate that the sight of *her* in her red silk dress had rendered him just as speechless. She tried to guess what *he* was thinking as he took in every inch of her from her upswept hairdo down to her outrageously high red heels. By the look of the smouldering expression in those deeply set dark eyes of his, he was as aroused by her appearance as she was by his.

The thought sent her blood fizzing through her veins.

'I think the lime-green would have been preferable,' he muttered at last.

'As would your pin-stripes,' she countered drily.

His eyes clashed with hers and a wry smile lifted the corners of his mouth. 'Shall we skip dinner in favour of a late supper?' he drawled. 'A late...*late* supper?'

Justine hesitated. It was one thing to plunge into an affair with him when it had just been a matter of sex. Would she survive giving him her body in true love? This was a new experience for her in more ways than one. Frankly, it terrified the life out of her.

Marcus saw her hesitation and frowned. What was she playing at *now*? Was he to be teased some more, made to sit and wait over a long drawn-out dinner he had no appetite for? Was she hoping that by the time the big moment came he'd be so blind with lust and longing he'd promise her anything? Marriage, even?

This last thought brought him back to cold, hard reality with a jolt. There he'd been, worrying about her all week, about his own selfishly wicked intentions, about how she constantly seemed to be smashing all his preconceived ideas after her. He'd even begun to believe her feelings for him might be genuine, that she had no mercenary plans in mind.

But if that were true then she would not be hesitating now; she'd be wanting him as badly as he was wanting her. There would be no hesitation, no game-playing.

'If you're desperate for dinner,' he grated out testily, 'then we'll have dinner.'

'I...I'm not desperate for dinner...'

'Then what's the problem?'

'The problem? I...I guess I'm a little nervous,' she confessed.

Marcus sighed. He hadn't thought of that. No matter what her motives, she hadn't been to bed with a man before. He was so sure himself it would be fantastic that he hadn't stopped to think she might be worried about the outcome.

He picked up her hand and drew it to his mouth, pressing his lips to each fingertip. 'Trust me,' he murmured thickly, and felt his desire for her kick back to where it had been all week, tormenting him every minute of every day.

She didn't say a word as he drew her down the front path to the street, where he settled her into his car; nor on the twenty-minute drive to his house; nor in the time it took to guide her from the triple garage in through his front door.

She made no comment over his house, as luxurious as it was. There again, girls like her were used to luxury, he reasoned. They took such things for granted.

The first words she spoke came when he led her into the master bedroom and turned her to him.

'I won't sleep with you in the same bed as you slept with your wife.'

He was taken aback, both by her shakily delivered pronouncement and the obvious emotion behind it. Was it jealousy which inspired such a sentiment? He hoped it was. Jealousy was real, not contrived. Jealousy he empathised with. The thought of Justine going from his bed to any other man's brought such a black jealousy that he hadn't yet confronted its full meaning.

He pulled her into his arms, his mouth barely

inches away from her. Her eyes glittered and he saw her hunger matched his.

'It's not the same bed,' he growled. 'I bought a new one after I threw her out.'

'Oh,' she said. 'That's all right, then.' And, sliding her arms around his waist, pressed herself against him.

Marcus's mouth crashed down on hers, passion rampaging through him like a river in flood. It was a battle to control the primitive urge to rip the clothes from her body and surge into her where they stood. She didn't help when she moaned deep in her throat, or when her nails began to dig into his back.

He wrenched his mouth away at last to drag in a much needed breath, but his name on her lips brought him swiftly back. His hands shook uncontrollably as they moved to undo the single button at the back of the halter-necked dress. When he felt it give way he groaned, the knowledge that shortly she would be naked bringing a white-hot haze down over his brain. His already teetering control shattered totally. With a harshly primal cry, he scooped her up into his arms and carried her over to the bed.

Justine exulted in his animal-like force. This was what she wanted, what she needed. To be given no time to think or to worry. To be swept away on the passion of the moment.

She lay there, wide-eyed and head whirling, while he stripped her then joined her on the bed.

His hands stroked possessively over her nakedness, heating her flesh and her blood. She gasped under his caresses, then moaned, wriggled and writhed. Her legs fell wantonly apart, inviting more intimacies.

He knew exactly where to touch to drive her wild. And how to touch. His fingers eventually gave way to his lips, and finally his tongue. Her first climax brought cries and shudders. Her second, a tortured sob. Her third, pleas to stop.

He did. But not for long, stripping himself and drawing on protection in no time. Before her breathing even slowed a fraction he was looming over her, magnificent in his nakedness, awesome in his need. The memory of the pain he'd caused last time brought a moment of panic. So when he bent his mouth to her breasts instead, she sighed her relief.

But his tongue on her nipples soon brought moans, not sighs. He laved them mercilessly, then tugged at them with his teeth till they burned with a white-hot heat which blazed a furnace through the rest of her body. When he moved between her legs she was no longer thinking about pain, so great was her craving to be as one with the man she loved.

And there was no pain as his flesh fused with hers, despite his filling and stretching her to the full. Her legs automatically wound around his waist, their bodies becoming blended and moulded in a single unit.

Justine moaned softly when he began to move, then when he cupped her face and kissed her at the same time, his tongue surging in a parallel rhythm with his penis. It was so much more intimate than anything she could ever have imagined, so much more emotionally moving. She clung to him with her hands and her heart, then finally came with him.

'Oh, Marcus,' she cried, her mouth bursting from his as her body clenched and unclenched his in a series of deeply satisfying spasms. 'Darling Marcus…'

'Darling Marcus' didn't allow himself the pleasure of staying inside her after he was done, rolling from her before he ended up losing more than his control. But, dear God, she tugged at his heart, made him want to say stupid things, promise stupid things.

He got up immediately to stride into the bathroom and do what he had to do. Afterwards he glared in the vanity mirror and warned himself not to let her lack of experience corrupt his common sense. Virginity did not necessarily equate with innocence. Or ignorance. She still might be faking it.

But what kind of girl would fake what had happened out on that bed? Such a devious action didn't equate with the Justine he now knew: the daughter who loved her mother and her home with such a selfless passion; the girl who'd sold her car and her clothes to make ends meet; the proud and high-spirited creature who took a cleaning job rather than ask her wealthy lover for money.

Marcus scowled at his reflection, with its wary eyes and sour mouth. The trouble was he'd hugged his lack of faith in females to himself for so long it was difficult to give it up—difficult to be open to real feelings, difficult to accept the possibility that Justine might not be trying to manipulate him for her own ends.

Damn it all, he could not stand his suspicion and distrust any longer. It was getting in the way of what he wanted, which was Justine in his bed—not just for a night, but every night. He wanted her as he'd never wanted Stephany. And he wanted her to want him back the same way. Obsessively. Possessively.

Maybe it was love. Maybe it wasn't. Whatever, he couldn't turn his back on it any longer. He had to embrace it. Had to!

Justine could not feel sad as she lay there. Or even regretful. Making love with Marcus had been too wonderful to spoil it with negative thinking. He might not love her, or want to marry her, but she felt sure he liked her now. Maybe he even respected her a little these days. He certainly wanted her. There was no doubt about that in her mind.

The bathroom door opened and she turned to look at him. God, but he was lovely naked. A real man. Broad shoulders. Narrow hips. Long, muscular legs. And the most incredible chest, with a matting of soft dark curls in its centre.

Her eyes lifted to his and her stomach lurched. He'd looked at her with desire before, but this was something else. His narrowed eyes held hers as he came forward and lay down beside her and began to kiss and stroke her anew. Yet with a strangely restrained passion this time. There was nothing remotely rough in his lovemaking this time. His touch was gentle, his mouth teasing, his tongue softly tantalising.

Slowly, skilfully, he rekindled the fires within her, taking her to that point of no return where her own passion took over and *she* became the aggressor, pushing him onto his back and bending her mouth to him as he had to her.

* * *

Marcus gasped when her lips brushed over his straining flesh, clutching at the quilt lest he go all noble and stop her. He hoped and prayed that the part of him which ached to surrender mindlessly to her own seemingly mindless passion would prove much stronger than the stupidly spoiling feelings which kept besieging him. This was what he wanted, wasn't it? For her to be so turned on, so carried away that she would do anything he asked of her, anywhere, any time? Such a scenario had plagued him ever since he'd met her. He wanted it. Hell, he needed it. Only then would this madness have a chance to burn itself out and leave him in peace.

He didn't want to love her. He wanted it to be nothing but lust. A passing passion. A quenchable fire.

Her lips were moving intimately over him and everything inside him lurched.

Dear God, girl, don't do it, he found himself thinking in an agony of ambivalence.

For at the back of his mind, in that place reserved for the harshest of truths, he knew if she did, if she took him into the heat of her mouth, if she reduced him to a screaming, mindless mess this way, then he would be lost in her for ever.

He moaned when her lips parted, groaned when she started to take him in. The physical sensation was delicious, the emotional impact devastating. She was doing it. Dear God...

His muscles tensed as he fought the tempestuous feelings which threatened to overwhelm him. But he was powerless against her passion, and his own. *She* was supposed to become *his* victim. Instead, he was on the verge of being the vanquished one. A slave to her superior will. Hers, in love and in lust.

Her mouth and hands were masterful, and merciless. They brooked nothing but his total surrender.

Marcus fought the good fight for what felt like an interminable time. Perhaps it was only a minute or two. She stopped for a second, giving him a moment's respite, making him think he might survive this after all. But then she glanced up at him, blowing him away with the look of blind adoration in her passion-filled eyes.

Now, instead of stopping her, he urged her back to his burning flesh and just let go of everything he'd been battling to contain. His body. His heart. His very soul.

CHAPTER FOURTEEN

MARCUS stood beside the bed, staring down at her nude body. She was curled up in a foetal position, her left arm covering her perfect breasts, her lovely hair spread out on the pillow, the curve of her bare bottom looking childlike.

Yet there'd been nothing childlike in the way she'd responded to him. She'd been all woman.

How many times had he had her already? He'd lost count. He'd imagined making love to her countless times might rid his body both of his passion for her and those other more disturbing feelings.

It hadn't worked. He was still flooded with the same emotional weakness every time he touched her. There really wasn't any point in denying it any longer. He loved her.

So what are you going to do about it, Marcus?

He didn't know yet. There was no rush to do anything, he supposed. No reason to reveal this unexpected development in their relationship. He really needed time to think about his feelings further, time away from the corrupting and confusing influence of her flesh.

His gut crunched hard as he thought of how that flesh felt. He really could not get enough of it. He walked around the foot of the bed, his gaze still hungry upon her.

But enough is enough, Marcus, he lectured himself. Besides, it won't work. Even when it's over, you'll still want her again. And again. And again.

It was going on three o'clock. They'd been making love on and off for several hours, their torrid matings punctuated only by coffee and a couple of revitalising swims in the pool. They hadn't eaten anything except each other. Their conversation had been the talk of lovers. Basically empty but complimentary. Flattering. His especially.

Of course he hadn't told her he loved her. Neither had she even come close to saying the same in return. But he was in no doubt that her sexual feelings for him were real. The mechanics of orgasm could be faked, he knew. But not the gush of liquid heat which flooded her. Neither could she engineer the way her nipples lengthened and hardened at his touch, or the way her eyes would darken and grow heavy.

He didn't think a faker would be quite so accommodating, either. There was nothing he'd demanded that she hadn't done with an abandon which had stunned and enthralled him.

He groaned at the memory, grimacing as he felt his body begin to ache one more amazing time. He really had to wake her and take her home. But he couldn't. Just thinking of her responses had him lying down beside her and stroking her silky flanks till she uncurled on a low moan and snuggled against him.

'It's late,' he murmured, and kissed her on the shoulder.

'Mmm,' was all she said, and she kissed him on the chest.

'I really should take you home, Justine.'

'I don't want to go home.' She licked at a nipple, then nibbled at it till he gasped.

'I want to stay here with you for ever,' she sighed against his skin.

Marcus frowned. Was this the first sign of plan B? He decided to test her.

'What do you mean?' he asked carefully. 'Are you saying you want to move in with me?'

Her head shot up, her hand pushing her hair out of her face. 'Good heavens, no. I can't do that. I have a boarding house to run. I didn't get round to telling you, but we had so many enquiries today from the ad in the *Herald*. I could fill each of those rooms ten times over. It was just a…a wish, that's all. I know I have to go home.'

Perversely, he felt disappointed. If she was in love with him, she would jump at the chance. If she had marital designs on him, she'd be doing cartwheels!

He almost wished she *did* have designs on him.

'What if I asked you to?' he said, and waited in an agony of anticipation for her answer.

She sat up and blinked at him. 'But why would you do that? I wouldn't have thought you'd like that idea at all.'

Hardly the answer of one besotted. No, *he* was the only fool around here who was besotted!

'I don't see why not,' he drawled, and reached out to tweak her nearest nipple, his male pride soothed by the sight of its instant response. If nothing else, she was in lust with him at least.

Or was it lust itself she was enamoured of? That newly discovered dark side of herself which could drive one to go to the bed with the strangest partners? Since Stephany's departure Marcus had found carnal solace in the arms of women he hadn't particularly liked. Maybe Justine was doing the same.

The thought that she might not particularly like him at all was quite crushing.

'What is it that you want of me, Justine?' he was driven to ask. 'What are you expecting from our relationship?'

Justine heard the edge in his voice, and the emphasis on the word 'expecting'. Oh, dear heaven, he thought she was angling for marriage. As much as she loved the man, marriage had not even entered her head!

How could it when she already knew marriage was the last thing Marcus wanted? Trudy had warned her of this, warned her not to fall in love with him. If he had even a hint of her true feelings, she wouldn't see hide nor hair of him again.

The concept of never making love with Marcus again, of never experiencing what she knew only he could make her feel, brought forward a brutally pragmatic response to his question. Better she lie than lose him. Better she fulfil the role he wanted her to play than have no part in his life at all.

'Expecting, Marcus? I'm not sure what you mean. I'm not expecting anything from you but what you offered.'

'And what was that?'

'Your friendship. And your body, of course,' she added with a saucy little smile.

'My body...'

She stroked down his chest and over his half-erect penis, her heart leaping along with his flesh.

It was still hard to believe how love had changed her perception of sex. She found it all so delicious. Nothing embarrassed her with Marcus. Everything seemed perfectly natural yet at the same time unbearably exciting. She loved the feel and taste of his body, loved arousing him, loved hearing him groan and tremble deep within her.

He rolled away from her and sat up on the side of the bed. 'Tell me about plan B,' he grated out.

Shock tripped her tongue for a moment. 'Plan...B?'

His glance over his shoulder was harsh.

'Please don't act obtuse. Felix mentioned your plan B on the night of his party. He implied I was the first cab off the rank.'

She stared at him, her heart hammering in her chest. Dear God, had he been thinking all the while that she was trying to ensnare him into marriage? Did he believe the things she'd been doing in this bed tonight had been inspired by greed and not genuine feelings? Had he demanded and enjoyed such intimacies with her suspecting she was nothing but a cold-blooded ambitious little bitch?

If he did, then he could go to hell!

'Firstly, it wasn't *my* plan,' she ground out in an agony of dismay and disappointment. 'It was Trudy's. Some ridiculous idea she had about my catching myself a rich husband. At one stage she thought you might be a suitable candidate, but I soon set her straight about that, believe me.'

He had the hide to actually look offended! 'You don't think I'm suitable husband material?'

'You have to be joking. You're far too bitter and

cynical about women. A woman would have to be crazy to want you as her life's partner.'

'Is that so?'

'Yes. When I marry it will be to a man who loves me to pieces and thinks I'm the best thing since sliced bread. A man who would never question my motives because he knows I love him back the same way. I've seen first-hand what happens when someone marries for money, not love. I want no part of such a sick bargain.

'So, do stop worrying, Marcus darling,' she flung at him, barely controlling her temper. 'I have no designs on you personally, or on your bank balance. I just want your body. But if you're not careful, I might not want that any more, either. I'm sure I will very shortly develop an aversion to being intimate with a man who thinks I'm nothing but a gold-digging tramp!' She scrambled off the bed and began scooping up her clothes from the floor.

'Justine,' he said frantically as he followed her around the room. 'Please don't be angry. I'm sorry. I...'

'Oh, I'm not angry!' she spat at him before he could voice a single more insincere word. 'I'm bloody furious! To think I waited this long, just to give my virginity to a cynical bastard like you!'

When she went to brush past him on her way to the bathroom, he grabbed her upper arms and forced her to face him, her bundle of clothes a convenient barrier between their naked bodies. Temper, it seemed, was no barrier to desire. Or love. Justine could not believe she still wanted the man!

'You're right,' he growled. 'I *am* bitter and cynical about women. I admit it. And I hate it as much as you do. Hate the stupid, narrow-minded, prejudiced view I formed of you the very first night I saw you.'

Justine was taken aback. But it hadn't been *night*, the first time they'd met. What on earth was he talking about?

'Yes. I see you're confused. I'm not talking about that day you came into the bank. I'd seen you once before that—at one of Felix's parties. Last November, it was. You wouldn't have seen me. I was inside, with Felix. You were frolicking in the pool, surrounded by young male admirers.'

'And?'

'I watched you for a while…'

Justine remembered that night very well, since it had been the night her father died. She vividly recalled being in that pool, recalled Howard's silly antics, pulling down her top underwater. She especially recalled flouncing out of the pool like the spoilt little miss she'd been back then.

She thought of Marcus watching her and her cheeks pinkened with embarrassment. 'I suppose I looked pretty silly,' she said.

'I thought you looked incredibly beautiful,' he said, dark eyes gleaming hotly. 'I wanted you so much it was almost unbearable. Felix noticed my fascination and said he'd introduce me to you, but I chose to leave instead. I'd already tagged you as another Stephany, you see…'

Justine's heart twisted at the pain in his eyes. 'She must have hurt you a lot, Marcus.'

'She destroyed my dreams.'

'Your dreams?'

'Yes. But that's another story, and not one you'd

be interested in. I'm simply trying to explain that when you came into my bank that day I was programmed to believe the worst of you. Not that that made any difference to my wanting you,' he added ruefully. 'If anything it seemed to make things worse. Instead of despising you, I desired you even more. I was severely tempted to abandon every standard I valued for just one night with you.'

'Goodness!' she exclaimed.

'Well, I've had my one night now and I want you more than ever. I adore everything about you, Justine. Your enthusiasm for life. Your spontaneity. Your passion.'

'Don't you mean sex?'

'That, too. Marry me, Justine. Marry me.'

She gaped up at him. 'Marry you! But I...I can't!'

'Why not?'

'Because...because if I do, you'll destroy *my* dream.'

'What's that? Your boarding house plan? Good God, Justine, as my wife you won't have to bother with that. I'll clear your debts. Hire your mother a housekeeper. Neither of you will have to worry about a thing for the rest of your lives.'

Justine wanted to slap his arrogantly insensitive face. Couldn't he hear himself? He was no better than her father, or Stephany. No talk of love, just money. She resisted the urge to cry, or scream, settling for straight talk instead.

'No, Marcus,' she said firmly. 'You've got it all wrong. My dream has nothing to with houses. It's about love.'

'Love?'

'Yes. You sound as though you've never heard of it, despite it being a four-letter word! The fact is, Marcus, I promised myself I would never marry except for love. *True* love. Not simply to fulfil a sexual attraction. I'm sorry, but you…you just don't fill the bill.

'Thank you for asking,' she raced on blithely, before she could do anything stupid like cry. 'But it really wasn't necessary. Men who deflower virgins don't have to marry them in this day and age. I'm sure once you think about it later you'll be relieved I didn't take you up on your impulsive offer. After all, you don't love me, Marcus. You simply want to make love to me, which you can still enjoy, quite frequently and free of charge, without the encumbrance of a wife. Because I like making love to you too, darling. You're as great in bed as I thought you'd be. Now I'm going to have a shower and get dressed. Then I think you'd better drive me home before Mum comes after you with a shotgun.'

Marcus stared, wide-eyed, after her retreating nakedness, his head whirling with a perverse joy.

She'd knocked him back. Told him where to stick his offer of marriage, *and* his bank balance. She was nothing like Stephany. Nothing at all!

Except in that she doesn't love you, you fool, the ugly voice of brutal honesty piped up, dampening his exuberance a little. You heard her. She'll only marry for true love.

Then he'd have to make her fall in love with him, wouldn't he?

But how?

Sex? Oh, yes, he'd use sex…at every opportunity. He thought she was great in bed, did she? Well, he aimed to be great *out* of bed as well. She ain't seen nuttin' yet!

Attention? He'd ring her up twice a day.

Presents? He'd send her flowers. Bring chocolates and perfume every time he called. Whoops, no! He didn't want to give the impression he still thought her a gold-digger. Just flowers, then. And nothing over the top.

Flattery? He didn't need to use flattery. He would just tell her the truth—that he thought she was the most beautiful, clever, witty, entertaining, wonderful, fantastic sexy female who'd ever drawn breath!

But what about that old standby…telling her he loved her every other sentence?

Now why was it that Marcus feared that particular truth wouldn't work? No, he would keep those three little words in reserve till the moment was right, till something happened and Justine would see that he really meant them. Then and only then would that tack have a chance of striking home!

Marcus's jaw jutted out stubbornly. He'd overseen plenty of mergers and takeovers in his life. But none as crucial as this. Nothing inspired him more than a difficult challenge. And he had a feeling that making Justine fall in love with him was going to be just that. But making her believe he loved her back might prove to be the emotional equivalent of *Mission Impossible*!

But when Marcus Osborne set his sights on an objective, it had better watch out. He wasn't the youngest bank president around for nothing!

He was bending to scoop up his own clothes when he heard the shower running.

The thought infiltrated that showers were filled with all sorts of erotica. Naked bodies, warm water, shower gel, sponges, back scrubs...

Marcus dropped his trousers and strode towards the bathroom door.

CHAPTER FIFTEEN

'I'LL BE sad to lose you,' Pat said over their eight-thirty cup of tea the following Friday night. 'You're a good little worker, Justine. Make someone a good little wife one day.'

Justine rather agreed with her. But she doubted Marcus ever would. He hadn't repeated his first impulsive proposal of marriage. He'd been too busy taking advantage of her offer to provide him with sex. Gratis. Naturally he had no idea she was in love with him. He thought she was just in lust with him—which, of course, she was as well.

On Sunday evening he'd returned to take her out to dinner again, and they'd actually made it to the restaurant this time. They'd eaten a couple of courses, though for the life of her Justine could not remember what. The sexual tension between them had been distracting in the extreme, both of them falling awkwardly silent during the drive back to Marcus's place.

They hadn't made it to the bed. Marcus had pounced on her in the hallway. She'd had great difficulty finding her clothes afterwards. They'd been scattered through the house. Her panties by the front door. Her lime-green dress beside the leather sofa in the lounge room. Her soggy bra out on the terrace.

Monday, he'd talked her into meeting him for lunch—only of course it had been *she* who was on his menu. She'd chided him when he'd headed home instead of to any eating establishment, but any mild reproach on her part had soon changed to a passion as driven and conscienceless as his.

Tuesday, she'd been breathlessly waiting for him outside his house when he drove up shortly after one, as arranged. The day had been steamingly hot and they'd spent two hours in the pool, making love. It was after three by the time Marcus went back to the bank, with an exhausted Justine left to wonder at his amazing stamina and imagination.

Wednesday, she'd refused to meet him for lunch, a perverse jab of pride demanding she not be so easy. But it had been darned difficult. She'd been on edge all day, the continuing hot weather not helping. She'd kept thinking how she would prefer being in Marcus's pool, with a deliciously naked Marcus, rather than washing sheets and making up beds for the coming boarders. By the time she'd arrived at work that night she'd been deeply regretting her decision. Why deny herself the pleasure Marcus could give her? If she couldn't have his love, then at least she could have his lovemaking.

When she'd wheeled her cleaning trolley into his office to find him sitting at his desk, looking supersexy, despite his wearing that stuffy pin-striped suit of his, she'd surrendered to the devil's whispers and seduced him on the spot. She still blushed at the thought of what she'd done under his desk, with people walking down the corridor a few feet away.

As much as Justine had enjoyed these erotic encounters, *nothing* compared to what had happened on Thursday.

Thursday, Marcus had taken her to an extravagant lunch in a swanky hotel on the Harbour, then up to a room afterwards—'For some leisurely afternoon lovemaking,' he'd said. His call to Grace to excuse his presence from the bank for the rest of the day had been a classic of *double entendre*. He'd told his secretary that he'd run into a valued client over lunch who had an exciting new proposition for him, and that he'd be all tied up for the afternoon.

Justine had had no idea at the time that he'd meant it literally. He'd seen it in a movie once, and found the idea a serious turn-on.

'Provided, of course, one's partner can be totally trusted,' he'd murmured as he'd kissed her into compliance against the hotel room door.

Justine shook her head as she thought of that afternoon. Having him at her total mercy had been corruptingly exciting. And surprisingly informative. She'd revelled in being able to tease him, in taking him to tantalising and probably torturous edges, at which point she'd coaxed answers to questions he would probably have sidestepped if he hadn't been desperate with desire. Acute frustration had allowed her to strip away the controlled façade he usually hid behind, and all sorts of interesting facts had come tumbling out of his groaning mouth.

During the course of the afternoon Justine had elicited quite a chunk of his life story. She'd been both fascinated and moved. Born to a drug-taking teenage runaway—father unknown—he'd been taken from his mother at a tender age by welfare and well-meaning relatives, and put into a wonderfully warm and welcoming state institution.

There had been no hope of adoption with his mother refusing to sign any papers, although he'd been fostered out several times to people who'd seemed more interested in their government cheques than the emotionally deprived boy. Finally he'd been consigned to the home for wayward boys after a bout of bad behaviour which came after news of his mother's death through an overdose— news which had shattered his secret dream of one day having a family of his own.

Naturally, as soon as he'd finished school he left the boys' home, to make his own way in the world. He'd worked his way through university, after which he'd joined the bank as a trainee loans officer. Twelve years later, he'd become the president of said bank.

Justine smiled ruefully at the memory of Marcus's modestly succinct description of his success. To rise to his present position in such a short time had been quite spectacular.

Actually, she knew more about his working history than he knew she did. Trudy had played detective for her this past week, finding out from various sources all she could about Marcus Osborne, banker extraordinaire.

Apparently, during the eighties, he'd been one of the only investment executives to advise his bank not to lend money to the scores of flashy entrepreneurs who'd besieged most of the major banks and glibly conned them into handing over massive loans for speculative deals, but without proper security. When the property crash had come, Marcus had become his bank's golden boy, having saved them a fortune in bad loans. He'd been rapidly promoted, first to vice-president at the age of twenty-eight, then to president at thirty.

His only failure during those years, it seemed, had been his marriage, which had occurred soon after his promotion to president. According to Trudy's sources, Stephany had been the only daughter of another bank president, who hadn't been so fortunate in his decisions and had subsequently been sacked.

Suddenly impoverished, the spoilt only daughter of the family had turned her greedy eyes on the banking man of the moment. Marcus had married her before he knew the selfish soul behind those big and reportedly beautiful brown eyes. Their marriage had lasted only twelve months, with no children.

Justine was no psychologist, but she believed anyone with a brain in their heads could see Marcus's deprived upbringing had been the perfect breeding ground to produce a driven personality with an intense need to succeed in life. But resting alongside his tunnel-vision ambition would lie a deep well of emotional vulnerability.

Love would always present itself as a two-edged sword. He would distrust it, yet crave it as one always craved what one had never had. The only problem would be that he might not know what true love was. The poor darling had had little experience of it, after all.

How easy to confuse lust with love. Or to be fooled by a gorgeous young woman who lavished him with false affection and flattery while hiding her mercenary motives behind a beautiful and distracting façade. Stephany had obviously been just such a woman.

Justine frowned. Marcus had thought *she* was tarred with the same brush for a good while. She hoped he didn't still think that. Hopefully, he didn't. Surely her rejecting his proposal of marriage had shown him she wasn't after his money?

The one subject Justine hadn't been able to coax Marcus into talking about in any detail on Thursday was his marriage, other than admitting he'd divorced Stephany for adultery. Most of what she knew of Marcus's ex was what she'd learned from Trudy—which wasn't all that much. A sudden thought occurred to her, and she glanced at the woman opposite.

'Tell me, Pat, did you ever meet Marcus's... er...Mr Osborne's first wife?'

'Did I ever! Now there was a one. We all cheered the day the boss got rid of her, I can tell you.'

'How long ago was that, exactly?'

'Gosh, it must be nearly two years ago now. Yep. Two years. Heavens, how time flies!'

'What was she like?'

'Lovely to look at. Tall and blonde, with a spectacular figure. Butter wouldn't melt in her mouth around Mr Osborne and any of his business colleagues, but she was a right cow to anyone she considered didn't rate. A snob through and through. I used to clean the seventh floor back then, and I ran into Madam quite a few times times in the evenings. She always looked right through me, as though I didn't exist. Poor Grace used to complain about the way she was treated as well.'

'Do you know what broke up the marriage?'

Trudy had told her rumour claimed there had been more than one affair on Stephany's part, but Trudy hadn't known the particulars.

'No secret there, love. The boss caught her in

bed with the pool-cleaning man. He tossed her out on the spot. Threw all her clothes—and her—out into the street, then had the locks changed.'

'Goodness! But how do you know that for sure? I mean, I can't imagine Mar... Mr Osborne telling anyone anything so personal.'

'Heard it all with my own little ears. Mr Osborne had come back to the bank that evening to work, as was his habit most evenings back then, when Lady Muck came storming into his office and let fly. I was cleaning the boardroom at the time, and the adjoining door was slightly ajar. My ears went bright red, I can tell you. I've never heard such filthy language from a woman in all my life!

'I was right proud of Mr Osborne, though. He never raised his voice once. Just told her quietly to leave. It wasn't till she started screaming out really shocking details of all the other lovers she'd had since their marriage that he called Security and had her forcibly removed. We all felt so sorry for him, being publicly humiliated like that. Everyone on the floor must have heard. We're not surprised that there hasn't been anyone else since then. Mr Osborne is the sort of man who would feel something like that very deeply. I doubt he'll ever marry again. Before his disillusionment, the poor man was totally besotted with that creature.'

Justine's heart sank into a black pit. It was as she'd feared. Marcus would never get over his first wife enough to trust another woman, or to risk his happiness again. But it was crazy to be so upset about something she'd always known. Hadn't Trudy told her *ad nauseam*?

Justine sighed her dismay. Her silly romantic

soul must have been secretly hoping that some day
Marcus would fall in love with her and repeat his
offer of marriage.

'Why did you want to know, love?' Pat asked.
'Are you interested in our Mr Osborne?'

Justine was taken aback, although it was a fair
enough question. 'Oh. Er...well, he *is* a very good-
looking man, isn't he?'

'Oooh.' Pat eyed her knowingly. 'Now here's a
turn-up for the books. Of course *you're* a very
good-looking girl, too. Don't tell me the boss's
been giving you the eye while you've been up there
cleaning his office?'

'He *has* given me the odd second glance occa-
sionally,' she said, and tried not to look guilty. If
only Pat knew. The things that had gone on in the
boss's office on Wednesday night would have
turned more than her ears bright red!

Justine had expressly forbidden Marcus to work
late tonight. She wanted to do a really good cleaning job on her last night, or Gwen would be complaining when she came back the following
Monday and found poorly cleaned rooms.

But it had been lonely cleaning his empty office.
She missed Marcus. Not just his lovemaking, but
the man himself.

Her heart lurched at the sudden unbearable
thought that since he would never fall in love with
her, then one day he'd be gone from her life. He
would tire of her sexually and that would be that!

How on earth would she survive without him?
He'd become as essential to her as breathing.

Suddenly she wanted to cry. But that would
never do. Not in front of Pat. Plastering a false

smile on her face, she jumped up from the tea table. 'Must get back to work,' she announced brightly.

'But what about Mr Osborne?'

'What about him?'

'I mean…what are you going to do about you and him? I mean…this is your last night working here, you know.'

'Yes, I do realise that. I'm afraid I have to accept that Mr Osborne and I aren't meant to be, Pat,' Justine said, her heart catching.

Pat sighed. 'I think you could be right, love. That Stephany piece did a right good hatchet job on him. I wonder what happened to the rotten cow? Probably sailed on to some other rich sucker without a backward glance. Them types don't have a heart. Not like our Mr Osborne. Now, he's soft as mush under that stiff upper lip he likes to put on. Do you know, he sent Gwen flowers, and even visited her personally at home with the biggest box of chocolates? She was quite overcome. Not many bosses would do that for a cleaner.'

'No,' Justine said thoughtfully. 'They certainly wouldn't. Well, I'd better get back to work, Pat. See you later.'

'Yes, see ya, love. And don't be too upset about Mr Osborne. There'll be plenty of fellas for you in the years to come.'

But none that I'll want as I want Marcus, she thought wretchedly as she rode the lift up to the seventh floor. None that I'll love half as much. Justine knew in her heart that there would only ever be one true love for her.

Her mood lifted when she recalled what Pat had said about Marcus being soft as mush under his stiff upper lip. Maybe Pat and Trudy were wrong about his being so damaged that he would never fully trust or love a woman again. He'd asked her once what she wanted of him, but she'd never asked him what he wanted of her. Maybe because she'd been too afraid of the answer. Was it just sex he was looking for? Or could she hope he wanted more?

Trudy had told her to just enjoy the moment and not to hope for anything permanent. But Trudy was a bit of a cynic. She'd also insisted Justine not tell Marcus she was in love with him.

'He'll treat you like a doormat if he knows that,' she'd pronounced on the telephone earlier in the week. 'Truly, Jussie. I did warn you that you'd fall in love with the man once you went to bed with him, didn't I? You're like a babe in the woods when it comes to men and sex, especially men like Marcus Osborne. They eat little girls like you for breakfast. Now, you listen to your old friend, and hopefully you might get out of this affair relatively unscathed, plus a whole lot wiser. *Don't* go saying anything you shouldn't. That way, when he dumps you, you'll at least have your pride intact.'

Pride.

What was pride in the scheme of things if Marcus was no longer in her life?

Be damned with her pride! she decided.

The lift doors opened and she hurried down the corridor. Wasn't honesty worth a try? What if Marcus felt more for her than he'd let on and was just waiting for her to admit the same?

It was a possible scenario, given his background. He'd be wary of committing himself to another woman, especially one with a spoilt upbringing similar to Stephany's. His offer of marriage the other night might not have been a mad impulse of the moment. It might have been a blurted out expression of his deepest desire.

Maybe Marcus loved her...

Truly loved her.

Her heart swelled, then raced with the possibility. She had to know. And she had to know *now*! It would not wait another moment.

Bursting back into his office, she strode over to his desk and swept up his telephone. Punching in the number for an outside line, she then added his home number. She clutched the handpiece to her ear, counting the number of rings at the other end. Five. Six. Seven. Oh, please don't let him be out!

'Marcus Osborne.'

Now that he'd answered, Justine froze. This was a stupid idea. Stupid, stupid, stupid!

'Hello? Anyone there?'

'Marcus?' she squeaked.

'Justine? Is that you?'

'Yes...'

'What is it? What's wrong? Where are you? Aren't you supposed to be at work at the bank?'

'I am. I'm in your office.'

'Oh?'

'I...I *had* to ring you.'

'Well, I'm flattered. Not to mention frustrated,' he added dryly. 'Dare I hope you want me to dash over for a rendezvous in the storeroom? No? Damn. Guess I'll have to wait till tomorrow.'

'Marcus...'

'Yes, my love?'

Her heart twisted at the endearment. 'Am I?' she

choked out, her chest tightening. 'I mean *do* you? Love me, that is?'

Justine had heard of silences being described as deafening. Now she knew what they meant. Marcus's silence screamed through her head for several nerve-jangling seconds.

'Why do you ask?' he said at last, and her chest tightened another notch.

'It…it was important to me all of a sudden.'

'Why?'

'Because…because I want everything between us to be open and above board,' she blurted out. 'I hate thinking of the way we first met. I was worried you might still think I was after something from you.

'Which I am, of course,' she raved on, nerves making her babble uncontrollably. 'But it's not your money, Marcus. Or marriage. Although I wouldn't mind being married to you. Some day. But only if you loved me, of course, and wanted to marry me, because I…I love you, Marcus,' she finally confessed in a rush. 'That's what I'm trying to say. I love you. Oh, God…I hope you're not angry with me for saying so. Trudy said I shouldn't tell you, but…but I'm not Trudy, am I?'

Marcus struggled to control the emotion welling up in his heart, but it was a struggle he was destined to lose.

'No,' he managed at last in a strangled fashion. 'No, my darling, you're not anything like Trudy. And, no, I'm not angry with you, because I…I love you too. How could I not? Oh, God, Justine, I'm getting all choked up here.' He swallowed convulsively and dashed the wetness from the corners of his eyes. 'Do you have any idea how many years it's been since I cried?'

'You're crying?' She sounded dazed. 'Over me?'

'Over you.'

'You didn't cry over Stephany?'

'That bitch? God, no. Once I saw what she was made of I couldn't wait to have done with her.'

'What became of her, do you know?'

'Funny you should ask. I had no idea...till last Tuesday. Grace pointed out this article in the *Herald* to me about a New Zealand banker who was on trial for embezzlement. There was a photograph of his wife going into the court and it was Stephany. I was amused to read he claimed he'd been driven to the crime by his wife's excesses. I almost felt sorry for the poor devil. Leopards don't change their spots, do they? Stephany'll go to her grave conning men out of their money. You don't have to worry your pretty little head about her, Justine. I can't stand the woman. If she stood naked in front of me I wouldn't turn a hair.'

'But...but you must have loved her to begin with, Marcus.'

Marcus heard her insecurity and was tempted to lie. But she'd said she wanted everything to be open and above board between them. Best to start with the truth.

'I thought I did. As a young lad growing up I had this dream of one day having this perfect life, which included the perfect wife on my arm. Stephany played the role of perfect wife-to-be to perfection—till the ring was on her finger. I fell in love with the illusion she created, not the real woman underneath. She fooled me completely with her flattering words and ways. She was also an accomplished actress in the bedroom. I won't deny I was seriously infatuated in the beginning.

'I began to suspect something was wrong right from the honeymoon, when all she wanted to do was shop. By the time the crunch came, and I found out what she really was, the wool had already started slipping from my eyes. Still, for a long time after I discovered the truth about her, I mistook the hurt and bitterness I was feeling for a broken heart. More a bruised ego, I think. Once I fell in love with you, sweet thing, I saw that what I'd felt for her hadn't been true love at all, but a very poor copy.'

'I'm your true love?'

'The truest and the loveliest.'

'Oh, Marcus, now *I'm* crying!'

'With happiness, I hope?'

'Oh, yes.'

'I'm coming over.'

'Marcus, you shouldn't. I still have so much work to do. Please let me do it. I...I promise I'll come over to your place as soon as I've finished.'

'In that case you'd better ring your mum and tell her you won't be home tonight. It's going to take me hours to show you how much I love you.'

'Oh, Marcus... All right, darling. I'll ring and tell her straightaway.'

'She won't come after me with a shotgun, will she?'

'No, of course not.'

'Pity,' he muttered.

'What?'

'Nothing.' Marcus had thought Justine's love

was all he wanted. But it wasn't. He wanted more. He wanted her to be his wife and the mother of his children. And soon, not *some* day.

But she was still so young. He had no right to rush her, no right to insist she change all her plans to fall in with his. He would have to be patient, have to wait for her 'some day'.

Meanwhile…

'You won't change your mind about coming over?' he asked tautly, his body already in an agony of longing to hold her in his arms. 'Promise me.'

'I promise.'

Justine lay in Marcus's arms, listening to the rhythm of his sleep and thinking she had never been happier. Marcus had just made love to her with a passion and tenderness which had brought a different dimension to his lovemaking. There had been a sweetness to each kiss and caress which had touched her soul as well as her body. When he'd finally moved into her, telling her all the while how much he loved her, tears had welled up in her eyes. She'd clung to him afterwards, sobbing. He'd kissed the dampness from her cheeks and she'd seen the love for her shining in his eyes. She was, indeed, his true love, as he was hers.

Okay, so he hadn't asked her to marry him yet, but he would. Some day. When the time was right.

Justine knew that time might be a while coming. Marcus had been too hurt in the past to rush into anything. And, in truth, she wanted some more time to prove to him she was nothing like Stephany. She was actually looking forward to the challenge of running a boarding house, of finishing her degree part-time and completing what the last few months had set in motion—the transformation of Justine Montgomery from spoilt little rich bitch to a grown up and independent woman who could be proud of herself.

She never wanted to revert to being that other silly, empty-headed girl, who hadn't known the value of a dollar or how to do a full day's work. She almost felt guilty now of the way she'd treated Howard Barthgate, and those other boys she'd dated. She'd used them shamelessly.

Not that they had been guiltless. They'd all dropped her soon enough after her father's death, which just showed the depth of their feelings. Actually, boys like Howard Barthgate were a bit like her father, Justine believed. High on charm, but low on conscience. Marriage, to them, was often simply a merger for money. True love was a concept for peasants, and sex, a commodity to be found wherever it was available. She doubted there was a husband in her old social set who was faithful to his wife.

Marcus, on the other hand, was lower on charm but higher on conscience. Justine liked that balance a lot better. She sighed a deeply contented sigh and drifted into a deeply contented sleep.

Her happiness, however, was to be short-lived— disaster waiting with the dawn.

CHAPTER SIXTEEN

JUSTINE woke to the sound of wind, and a branch slapping its leaves on the bedroom window. The clock on the bedside chest said two minutes to eleven, which meant she was already two hours behind the hour she'd faithfully promised her mother she'd be home.

'Marcus,' she said, and nudged him in the ribs.

He groaned.

'Stay there if you like but I have to get up and go home. I have a lot to do today. Our first boarders are arriving tomorrow.'

Marcus yawned and stretched. 'God, what's that infernal noise?'

'It's the wind. But no rain, unfortunately. Clear blue sky again.'

'Crazy damned weather we're having. Almost as crazy as I am about you. Come here and kiss me good morning, you beautiful thing, you!'

'Oh, no, you don't!' Justine squealed, and warded him off. 'I have to get out of here in fifteen minutes or my mother is going to kill me. I promised her I'd be home long before this.'

Marcus grinned and snuck a quick kiss in. 'Was she shocked and horrified when you rang last night?'

'Mum? No. Mum's always let me run my own race. Nothing I do would ever shock her.'

'Wise Mum.'

'I don't know about wise. She's a bit on the scatty side, actually.'

'A darling, though.'

'Yes.' Justine sighed. 'Poor Mum. These last couple of months have been traumatic for her.'

'You underestimate her, Justine. She's a survivor.'

'Perhaps. I think Tom's in love with her.'

'The gardening chap?'

'Uh-huh.'

'Seemed a nice enough bloke.'

'He is.'

'What's the problem, then?'

'Mum was very much in love with Daddy. I don't think she'll ever fall in love again.'

'Funny. People said the same thing about me and Stephany…'

Justine looked sharply at him, and he grinned.

'They were dead wrong, weren't they? Now, off you go to the shower, my love, while I lie here and languish in the memory of last night.'

'Turn on the radio while you're languishing, lazy bones. See if you can get the weekend weather report.'

Twenty minutes later, a shocked Marcus was speeding up the Pacific Highway towards Lindfield, a pale-faced Justine sitting beside him. He hadn't just caught the weather, but the whole eleven o'clock news report. The newsreader's words were still ringing in his ears.

Some nut-case arsonist, not satisfied by the bushfires which had ringed the rural outskirts of Sydney all summer, had actually set fire to the National Park running along the Lane Cove River. Eighty-

mile-an-hour winds had whipped up what should
have been a containable blaze into an uncontrollable force, which was burning all in its path.

It seemed incredible that a bushfire should be
threatening homes in the inner city area, but that
was what was happening, according to the news.
Several houses had already been burnt to the
ground. Lindfield had been one of the suburbs
named where houses had succumbed, and more
were in danger. Since Justine's home backed on to
the park, Marcus feared it would be one of the first
at risk!

Justine's panic increased as Marcus drew nearer her
street. The pall of green-black smoke in the sky was
appalling. She hoped it was just the result of trees
burning, but feared this was an optimistic view. The
thought of her home burning to the ground was bad
enough. The fear of her mother in danger brought
a clutch of nausea to her stomach.

Marcus tried to keep a handle on his fear but it was
difficult. Things didn't look good.

Dear God, he prayed, as he hadn't prayed since
he was ten years old. Don't let anything happen to
Justine's mother. Or that stupid damned house. I
promise if you keep them both safe, I won't press
or coerce Justine into a precipitous marriage. I'll
even keep using protection and not have any convenient lapses of memory.

He couldn't drive down her street. It was blocked
with police cars.

Marcus knew without having to be told that the
situation was critical. He could actually see the

flames of one house burning at the far end of the
street. It *was* on the other side from Justine's home,
but with the wind it wouldn't take much to jump
that small distance. The sudden realisation that the
wind was going in the opposite direction and had
already done its business on the other side made
him quake inside.

'Oh, Marcus,' was all Justine said, despair in her
voice.

He parked his car down a side street and they
both ran back to the corner of Justine's street, where
groups of people were huddled behind a police barrier, everyone looking shell-shocked.

Justine suddenly grabbed his arm. 'Marcus!
Look, there's Mum! She's all right. Oh, thank God.'

Marcus did. But there was still the question of
the house. Lord knows what would happen if the
darned thing *had* burned to the ground. Adelaide
would probably fall apart and so might Justine. She
was a far more sensitive and sentimental girl than
he'd ever imagined, as evidenced by the sudden
flood of tears in her eyes.

'Don't cry, Justine,' he advised sternly. 'Your
mum doesn't need to see you crying. You have to
stay strong for her, darling, especially if something's happened to the house.'

'Yes—yes, you're quite right, Marcus,' she said.
'Mustn't cry. Must stay strong. It's only a house,
after all. Mum's fine. That's all that matters.'

He was so proud of the way she pulled herself
together, of the determination in her eyes to be
strong and brave for her mother. But he kept a comforting arm around her waist as they moved over to
where her mother was arguing with a policeman.

She didn't sound at all scatty, Marcus thought suddenly. She sounded like a mother frantic about her daughter, but determined to get answers. The policeman was looking very harried.

'But you *must* let me go down there, you stupid man. My daughter said she'd be home first thing this morning and Justine is as good as her word. I won't do anything silly, I promise. But I need to know if my daugh—'

Adelaide whirled when Justine tapped her on the shoulder, saying, 'Mum,' at the same time.

The look in the woman's eyes told it all, and Marcus knew that there was nothing on this earth like a mother's love. He felt momentarily sad for what he'd missed out on, then glad that the woman who would bear his children one day had been reared by a mother as caring as this.

'Oh, Justine!' Adelaide cried, her two chins wobbling. 'I've been so worried.' She clutched at Justine's upper arms, then hugged her tight. 'But you're all right. Tom, look, she's all right. My precious darling is all right.'

'Yes, dearest,' Tom said, coming forward from where he'd been silently standing by.

Justine stared at him when he slipped his arm around her mother's shoulders, her eyes widening when Adelaide slumped submissively against him. The mother tigress of a moment ago was gone, Marcus saw, replaced by the persona Adelaide had long since adopted, that of the fragile female who had to be cosseted and protected from reality.

'The house is gone, Justine,' Tom informed them both.

'Oh, God,' Justine choked out, and Marcus

steadied her with a squeeze. 'Were...were you able to get anything out?'

'I'm afraid not. By the time we got here they wouldn't let us down there. The street had been evacuated and blocked off.'

'What do you mean, when you got here?' Justine looked from Tom to her mother, then back at Tom.

Adelaide blushed while Tom straightened, his eyes clear and unwavering. 'Your mother stayed the night at my house, Justine.'

Marcus might have been amused by Justine's shock at any other time but this. 'She...she what?' she gasped.

'Your mother and I are in love, Justine,' Tom said, with a simplicity which was quite touching, Marcus thought. He liked the man. He was going to be a lot better partner for Adelaide than the likes of Grayson Montgomery.

'In love,' Justine repeated rather blankly.

'Yes, dear.' Her mother joined in at last, looking half-sheepish, half-defiant. 'Like you and Marcus. We're going to be married. Tom asked me last night and I said yes. The wedding will be quite soon. At our age we see no reason to wait.'

'But...but what about the house?'

Adelaide looked wistful, but not too distraught. 'It's very upsetting, I know, and I feel for you dreadfully. I know how attached you were to it, and how hard you fought to keep it.'

Marcus could feel Justine's dismay and frustration through every pore of her body. He knew full well she'd fought to keep the house more for her mother than for herself!

'It's only a house after all, dear,' Adelaide added.

'And it *was* heavily insured. Marcus made sure of that before he sanctioned the loan. Tom said I can move in with him straightaway. I doubt anyone will be scandalised in this day and age.'

'But...but what about your things? What about Grandma's jewellery?'

'All my mother's jewellery is in the bank's vaults—didn't I tell you? Marcus said if I wasn't going to wear any of it then I'd better put it somewhere safe since we were going to invite a lot of strangers into the house. Oh, my goodness, I'd forgotten about that! What are those poor students going to do when they find out their rooms no longer exist?'

'I dare say they'll survive,' Marcus said dryly. And so will you, Adelaide dear, he thought, though I'm not so sure about your daughter. She was looking stunned, the poor darling. She'd lost her home and her illusions in one and the same day.

'I think, Tom, that we should take Adelaide and Justine back to your place,' he advised. 'There's nothing any of us can do here for now. I'll speak to the policemen and find out when we can return.'

Tom's house proved a surprise. Only a few streets away, it was spacious and elegant with a magnificent garden. Tom confided over tea and cake that he hadn't always been a gardener. He had once been a middle-management executive for a large food company, but had been retrenched at fifty-one after his company was taken over. Despite a lucrative golden handshake he hadn't wanted to retire, and had gone into gardening—more as an interest than a career. It was apparent Adelaide would not want for anything by marrying him, either in affection or security.

Marcus was pleased to see Justine looking a little more her old self after an hour or so, though it was clear she was still far more distressed than her mother over the house. Her face was pale and there was a haunted look in her eyes.

He didn't think it was doing her much good being with her mother. Adelaide had obviously shut the door on her old life and home—both mentally and emotionally—and kept talking about Tom and the future with a slightly insensitive optimism.

Marcus suspected that was her way of coping, but it wasn't Justine's. She needed to openly grieve the loss of her home, and everything that home represented. When Marcus whispered that they could go back and look at what was left of the house now, she nodded her agreement.

It was worse than he'd envisaged. A blackened, sodden shell. A fire truck was still there, and they were warned not to touch anything, although it was obvious the thick stone walls weren't in any danger of collapse. Nothing was salvageable inside, everything either reduced to ash, or melted and twisted into unrecognisable shapes.

'Oh, Marcus,' was all Justine said over and over as they picked their way carefully through the rubble, her voice breaking.

It wasn't till she stared up at where the staircase had been that she seriously began to cry. Marcus folded her to him and let her. She needed to cry, needed to let it all out, needed to grieve.

She was deathly silent during the drive home.

His, not Tom's. Marcus wasn't about to let her go back there. Not tonight.

He poured her a stiff drink on arrival and pressed it into her hands.

'Don't be angry with your mother, Justine,' he said as she drank it down.

'I'm not,' she said, sighing. 'Not really. She's only doing what she's always done. Putting her head in the sand and pretending everything will be all right. And it probably will be. Tom's a good man. She's obviously going to be very happy with him. It's just that I feel so desolate. I can't explain it. I have nothing left from my life there. No photographs or mementoes. Nothing. It's as though I don't exist any more.'

'Not exist? Oh, Justine, my love, you exist more than anyone I've ever met. You walk in a room and the air is instantly warmer, the light brighter. You have a living aura around you which is both captivating and enchanting. You *are* life. But I understand what you're saying. I would have dearly loved some photographs of my mother. But, be assured, there are more photographs of you and your past life around than you realise. All your friends will have some. Relatives. Old classmates. Photographers keep negatives for decades, and so do people. We'll get some photographs for you, my love. Meanwhile, I have a little surprise for you—something which I think might make you feel better.'

'What?'

'Seeing is worth a thousand words,' he said, smiling, and led her along the hallway to the large back room which had been empty till a week or so ago.

He opened the door and guided her in, watching as her eyes widened on a gasp of spontaneous joy.

Marcus would always remember that moment, the way her face went from a bleak sadness to blazing happiness in one split second.

'Grandma's things!' she exclaimed. 'Oh, I'd forgotten about them. Oh, Marcus, what a wonderful surprise!' And she ran around the room, touching everything with loving little strokes of her hands, laughing and crying at the same time.

'I won't even make you marry me to get them back,' he teased.

Her head shot up and a mischievous glint came into her eyes. His heart turned over. The girl he'd fallen in love with was back, as bright and bold as ever.

'Was that a proposal I just heard?' she asked saucily. 'Or a bribe? Marcus Osborne, you wouldn't be trying to corrupt me, would you?'

'Could I?'

She started to undulate towards him and his throat thickened. 'Not with things, my darling,' she murmured, reaching up on tiptoe to wind her arms around his neck and press herself against him. 'But make love to me like you did last night and I'll be yours for ever.'

'Is that an acceptance, or another bribe?'

'It's a promise.'

Justine was moved by the expression which came into his eyes. She realised then that her mother had

been right. Love was all that mattered. Not a house.
Or things. Love.

'Will tomorrow be too soon for the ceremony?'
he asked impatiently.

She laughed. 'I don't think a marriage can be
arranged that quickly. Not legally.'

'Where there's a will there's a way.'

'Then go to it—pronto. Meanwhile...'

She became his wife by special licence seven days
later—Marcus pulling all sorts of strings and claim-
ing a pregnancy as the reason for the undue haste.

As it turned out, technically, he hadn't lied. Their
first child—a daughter—arrived eight months and
three weeks later, just in time to move into the new
house Marcus had had built on the burned-out
site—a duplication of the original house from the
plans they'd found still lodged at the local council.

It was always a happy house, with a carved mahogany balustrade which the children slid down,
but only when their grandmother was minding
them. She never seemed to notice their misdemean-
ours—not like their mother, who was very strict.
None of them believed for a moment the stories
their father told of their mother being a wild child
who had played hookey from school, been an outrageous flirt and who'd worn tight, sexy dresses.
That wasn't *their* mother. No way. That had to be
some other person.

But when their parents found the privacy of their
bedroom at night, and the children were fast asleep,
something happened to their mother. In Marcus's
arms she became a different woman, a woman who

knew she was very lucky to have found her true love in life. They would have been very surprised to see the woman she became then. Very surprised indeed!